D1326097

This book is due ... on or before the last date shown
above; it may, subject to the book not being reserved by
another reader, be renewed by personal application, post, or
telephone, quoting this date and details of the book.

HAMPSHIRE COUNTY COUNCIL
County Library

♻ 100%
recycled paper

Alex was breaking her heart.

'I just want to go home,' Lucy said quietly. 'Away from this place. Back to England—'

'Away from me?'

She forced herself to look into his eyes. She couldn't go on like this. There was no future in this crazy relationship; deep down she knew that. Men like Alex Darcy didn't make commitments to girls like her.

'Yes,' she replied firmly. 'Away from you.' She squared her shoulders and held herself upright. 'Now, if you'd let go of my arm...'

Laura Martin lives in a small Gloucestershire village with her husband, two young children and a lively sheepdog! Laura has a great love of interior design and, together with her husband, has recently completed the renovation of their Victorian cottage. Her hobbies include gardening, the theatre, music and reading, and she finds great pleasure and inspiration from walking daily in the beautiful countryside around her home.

Recent titles by the same author:

PERFECT STRANGERS

LIVING WITH THE ENEMY

BY
LAURA MARTIN

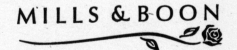
MILLS & BOON

MILLS & BOON and the Rose Device
are trademarks of the publisher.
Harlequin Mills & Boon Limited,
Eton House, 18-24 Paradise Road, Richmond, Surrey TW9 1SR

© Laura Martin 1996

ISBN 0 263 14948 X

Set in Times Roman 10 on 10½ pt.
07-9609-63580 C1

Made and printed in Great Britain

CHAPTER ONE

LUCY pushed her trolley past the lines of holiday-makers towards the airport exit. She felt anxious. But then, she thought ruefully, when didn't she?

Where was he? She stood awkwardly, trying not to look as if she were abandoned, but feeling dreadfully self-conscious amongst the bustle of people who streamed passed her and knew exactly where they were going.

Lucy's gaze flicked back and forward. She felt dishevelled and she longed for a cool shower and a good lie-down. No one seemed the least bit interested in her presence. She scanned the crowds for a face that might fit. Charles had been his usual vague self, and she hadn't thought in the rush of her departure to press for a description. Think, she told herself. What will he look like, this friend of Charles?

Her imagination did its best, but she had virtually nothing to go on. Most likely he would be of a similar type to her step-brother: heading towards middle age with a vengeance, medium height, medium weight, inclined to a paunch, maybe, from too much good food and not enough exercise.

I don't care what he looks like, Lucy thought, as long as he turns up soon and rescues me.

Worried emerald eyes rested hopefully on a kindly looking man with thinning hair who stood a few feet away. He looked as if he was waiting for someone, maybe... But not me, Lucy thought despondently as a brightly dressed woman and two young children rushed gleefully towards him. Try again.

Of course, the flight had been delayed and that hadn't helped the arrangement. Maybe Alex Darcy had got fed up waiting; maybe he had gone home. Maybe she would be standing here for the rest of the afternoon, looking and feeling like a lost soul...

'Lucy Harper?'

She turned at the sound of the voice. It surprised her: deep and mellow, with an edge of huskiness that sent an unexpected tingle down her spine.

'Yes?' She looked up, then raised her eyes another foot. Not medium height or medium weight, she thought as she looked into the deepest, darkest eyes that she had ever seen. Not medium anything.

'Hello, I'm Alex.'

His smile was wide and attractive. For a second Lucy stood bemused, looking up in wonder at her stunning companion. Black, glossy hair, a little longer than the norm, was swept back from a tanned, incredibly stunning face. Straight nose, high cheekbones, spiky lashes framing eyes which seemed to look right into her very soul...

All in all, it added up to something pretty special.

Lucy glanced down, disconcerted by Alex Darcy's direct gaze, saw his outstretched hand and offered her own, feeling a curious sensation as skin touched skin and contact was made. 'You were looking a little lost,' he murmured. 'Sorry I'm late. I went to the bar for a drink.'

'The flight...' She took a calming breath and managed a smile. 'It was delayed.'

'Yes.' Velvet eyes considered her with serious intent for a moment. 'You look tired. Come on, let's get out of here. It's chaos.'

He carried her bags outside. The warm, Mediterranean air was a welcome change after the cold, wet weather that Lucy had left behind in England, and as they walked across the tarmac to the airport car park she slipped off her knitted oatmeal jacket and draped it over her arm.

'Quite a difference in temperature, I should imagine,' Alex commented easily as he unlocked the doors of the sleek maroon Jaguar. 'Are you looking forward to your stay?'

Should she be honest? Lucy bit down on her bottom lip and decided that it wasn't the best policy. Not now, not so soon after meeting her host. 'Yes...' she murmured awkwardly, 'I'm sure it's going to be...very...nice.'

'You didn't want to come.' Dark eyes met hers over the sun-baked roof of the car. 'That's a pity.'

So this man, this friend of Charles, liked to be direct. Lucy swallowed and inhaled before replying. 'My stepbrother can be very persuasive,' she replied abruptly. 'I'm sure you're no happier about this arrangement than I am.'

Broad shoulders were lifted in an easy shrug. The white shirt he wore billowed a little in the warm breeze. It looked good against his bronzed skin, she thought. She felt pasty suddenly, and decidedly unhealthy in comparison with the glowing vitality which exuded from the man opposite.

'I have a large villa, a pool, a great view. You're welcome to share it with me for a few days,' he replied easily. 'Charles said you needed the break.'

'What else did he say?' Lucy's voice was sharp. She couldn't help it. Anxiety was always there, lying just beneath the surface, waiting to engulf her.

'Nothing much.' His voice was infuriatingly smooth. He looked at her without difficulty or embarrassment. 'I know that your husband died a couple of months ago and you need a change of scene.' He glanced around the car park and his mouth twisted into a smile. 'And here you are.'

Lucy's eyes rested on the shimmering concrete and the cars and the masses of people surrounding them. 'Yes,' she replied flatly. 'Here I am.'

She saw his look, a slight narrowing of his eyes, but he didn't say anything, not until they were in their seats and Lucy was fastening her seat belt.

'I live in the north. In the hills. You won't find fish and chip bars and high-rise hotels there,' he told her. 'It won't be like this.'

Wide emerald eyes met his gaze. Lucy didn't bother to hide her disbelief. 'Won't it?'

'No.' He thrust the car into gear and manoeuvred it out of the space. 'Be patient. You'll see.'

They travelled in silence for a long while. After an hour, the scenery changed to lush green trees and dusty tracks, to whitewashed houses nestling in valleys and clinging precariously to hillsides, and her heavy heart began to lift a little.

'Oh, it's so...so different!' she exclaimed, looking about her.

'There's still quite a way to go,' Alex informed her, refraining from the obvious comment of 'I told you so'. 'Do you want to stop for a while and stretch your legs? I have some cool drinks in the back.'

Lucy nodded. She had been feeling dreadfully thirsty for the last few miles and her legs felt old and unused. 'Yes,' she replied, grateful for the thoughtfulness of her companion. 'That would be nice.'

He clearly knew the area well. Alex drove the car to a quiet spot shaded from the afternoon sun by the branches of cooling trees. It was a wonderful relief to be able to get out and stretch and walk and just enjoy the fresh, clear air.

He handed her a drink from a cool-box in the boot and Lucy raised the cold bottle of cola to her mouth and drank thirstily.

'Tastes good?'

She lowered the bottle from her lips. 'Like nectar,' she replied shyly.

'You'll find that Majorca sharpens all your senses: sight, smell, taste... Take a deep breath,' he instructed. 'Wonderful, isn't it? So clear and fresh; sweet and sharp all at the same time.'

'And warm.' Lucy, conscious of Alex Darcy's gaze, turned to look at the view. The valley stretched endlessly ahead of them, with green terraces that glinted in the sun. In the distance the sea shimmered invitingly.

When Charles had first mentioned that she should go to Majorca to rest and recuperate Lucy had been aghast. He had talked her into it, as he always did, though, and now she could understand why. It was a magnificent part of the world.

Just a shame that this man...this stranger was part of the package. She would have much preferred to stay here alone. But Charles had been adamant about that...

'I need to know there's someone around—someone I can trust to look after you,' he had insisted firmly. 'Alex has certain...' he had hesitated a moment and then said '...qualities. Qualities that I feel I can rely on. I know you're well on the road to recovery, but—'

'You think it's fine for me to spend time in a house miles from anywhere, alone with a man I've never met before?' Lucy had asked from her wicker chair in the hospital garden. She'd shaken her head in disbelief. 'I'm really surprised that you should even make this suggestion!'

'Look, Alex is a good man. Anyway, he's a work-aholic!' Charles told her reassuringly. 'His writing is his life now. Honestly, he'll be sat in his study for hours on end, so you'll get all the peace and quiet you want. He'll be around—that's the main thing. I don't want you to feel abandoned. Alex has promised me he's perfectly happy for you to stay for a few days, just until I get this last-minute hitch sorted out. He'll understand.' He paused a moment. 'He might even be able to help you.'

'I doubt that!' Lucy threw the rug from her knees and stood up. 'And anyway, why should he want to? Not that I *need* help,' she amended swiftly. 'I feel fine. I don't want to stay with some man I've never met before. He could be...well, you know.'

Charles frowned and looked perplexed. 'Could be what? What do you mean?'

Lucy exhaled. 'Oh, Charles, you're so worldly in some ways and so totally naïve in others! I'll be alone, out in the middle of nowhere, with a man I've never met before—'

'Good gracious, Lucy! You really are clutching at straws!' Charles laughed. 'Is that the best reason you can give for not going?'

I'm nervous, Lucy wanted to say. I'm feeling fragile and I won't know him.

'Look, believe me,' Charles continued, 'you have nothing to worry about. Alex is a normal, red-blooded male who on occasion enjoys the company of women, but he's intelligent and humorous and totally absorbed in his work. Anyway,' he added tactlessly, 'they're never your type.'

'Who aren't?' She gazed down at her step-brother, puzzlement clouding her features. 'What are you talking about?'

'Alex's women,' Charles replied. 'I'm just trying to put your mind at rest; he doesn't go for your...' He saw Lucy's expression and his voice trailed away.

'And what exactly is my type?' she enquired, eye-brows raised.

'Oh, you know...' Charles waved a negligent hand.

'No, actually I don't!' she replied sharply. 'I've never met the man before, or had you forgotten?'

'Alex goes for glamour with a capital G. His women are usually six feet tall with hair the colour of corn,' he added wistfully.

'And as I'm a short five feet five inches, with a sprinkling of freckles and long, wavy red hair I'm safe— is that what you're saying?' Lucy shook her head. 'You know, for a diplomat you have a pitiful amount of tact!'

Charles looked uncomfortable. 'Now don't get worked up about it,' he added hastily. 'You're supposed to be keeping calm.'

'I am calm, you idiot!' she replied flatly. The edges of her mouth curved a little. 'I'm just disappointed that you won't be around. I see little enough of you as it is.'

Poor Charles, Lucy thought now, and wiped her moist forehead with the back of her hand. She loved him dearly, though. He was the best stepbrother in the world. The only relation close enough to matter. But she did, on occasions, give him a hard time. She heaved a steadying sigh. She wished he were here...

Her head was beginning to hurt. What was the last thing the doctor had said to her on her discharge from the hospital? What had Charles said to her at Gatwick when he had kissed her goodbye? 'Relax. Take it easy.'

'Are you feeling OK?'

Lucy looked up to find Alex close beside her. She took a step away, saw him frown and replied hastily, 'Yes... yes, I'm fine!'

'You don't look it.'

'I'm fine!' There it was again—that sharp, high-pitched tone that revealed her uncertainties and worries so effectively.

'You know, Charles really only has your best interests at heart. It will do you good to stay here a while.'

'Oh, yes?' Lucy raised her brows enquiringly. 'And you would know, would you?' She saw the firming of his mouth, wondered despondently what on earth was making her so disagreeable.

'I think so, yes.' His voice was crisp and well defined.

Lucy focused on the view. 'I didn't ask to come here. If I had had my way I would have gone straight home from the... the...'

'Hospital? You can say the word, you know,' Alex drawled. 'It won't bite.'

'I'd... I'd prefer to put all that behind me,' she replied stiffly, glancing across at him. 'If you don't mind.'

'Not at all.' The rich dark eyes held her gaze. 'You know, Lucy, there's no need to feel awkward about anything, or uptight. You're supposed to look upon your stay here as a holiday,' he continued with infuriating ease, 'not as some sort of incarceration.'

'I didn't want to come!' she said stonily. She glanced down and saw that her linen trousers looked grubby and crumpled. She smoothed the fabric against her legs with shaking fingers, conscious that the humiliation of tears wasn't far away.

'You preferred the idea of returning to your cramped little bedsit in the heart of London?' Dark brows were raised with an infuriating lack of sympathy. 'A rather depressing area by all accounts. You know that Charles wishes you'd find somewhere better? He thinks—'

'I know what he thinks!' she cut in. 'He's told me enough times.' She turned away angrily and stared out across the lush green valley. She felt hot and irritable and unreasonably defensive. Charles, it seemed, had told Alex more than she had imagined. 'Anyway, my "cramped little bedsit" suits me fine!' she added tightly. 'Besides, it's all that we could—that *I* can afford!' she corrected herself swiftly. 'I'm not into charity,' she continued, hardening her voice and her heart, pushing away the dull thud of misery which threatened to take a hold all over again whenever she thought of the mess that had been her marriage. 'I want to be independent. I was *going* to be independent, until Charles foisted me off onto you! He's just salving his conscience!' she continued. 'Charles is too busy to spare me any of his precious time and so he's come up with this ridiculous idea!'

There was an uneasy silence. Lucy raised a hand to her head and smoothed slender fingers across her aching brow. She knew that she would regret this later, this petulant outburst. What was wrong with her? Why was she acting so dreadfully?

'Tell me something.'

She glanced across, pushing a heavy strand of bronze-coloured hair out of her eyes, watching the handsome contours of Alex Darcy's face warily. 'What?'

'Are you always this ungrateful?' His voice was clipped and cool. There was almost a hint of dislike in his tone. Her eyes widened in surprise. 'Charles is doing the best he can,' he continued evenly. 'You know better than I how important his job is. He has commitments that cannot be broken. He's been working hard on the details of this summit for several months, hasn't he?'

'For about a year,' she replied flatly, knowing deep down that her stepbrother was doing his best, knowing that she was being difficult merely to cover her unease at being in this new situation with a man who was everything she hadn't expected.

'Well, then, surely you can understand his predicament?' Alex continued. 'He told me you were incredibly proud of his achievements. Not many men or women reach such a position so early in their career. Don't you think it's time you considered the difficulties Charles has to deal with, instead of thinking only of yourself?'

It was a shock to be put in her place. So many people had been treating her with kid gloves for so long that she had forgotten what it was like to be on the receiving end of someone's displeasure . . . almost.

'Thinking of myself—?' Lucy began. She caught sight of the watchful expression and released a weary sigh. 'OK, I'm sorry! I didn't mean to take any of this out on you.' It took a huge effort to keep her voice steady and calm. 'I just feel that Charles has treated me like a child. There was practically no discussion about my coming here,' she continued. 'One minute I'm in the hospital; the next I'm being informed that I'm to travel to Majorca to recuperate with an old friend who just happens to be a man, who just happens to be someone I've never met before.' She narrowed her emerald eyes. 'How would you feel?'

'A little disorientated, maybe, but essentially glad.'

'Glad?' She shook her head in disbelief.

'You *liked* hospital?' Alex enquired bluntly.

She hesitated, disliking the turn that the conversation was taking. 'No...not really.'

'You don't seem too sure.'

Lucy heaved a sigh. Losing Paul had been hell. The agony she had gone through over his death, the guilt... Oh, how it had affected her. A nervous breakdown was not a thing she ever wanted to experience again—ever! But the hospital had been her saviour. For those vital few weeks the anxieties of life had been taken out of her hands. She had been nurtured and cosseted; everyday decisions that had become so hard to deal with had melted away.

For the first time Lucy allowed her gaze to rest calmly on the handsome face. 'It was...safe,' she replied simply. 'There's a certain comfort in that.'

He looked at her in silence for a moment then took a step towards her, narrowing the space she had put between them. His eyes were dark and magnetic. A hand was raised slowly and for a moment Lucy thought that the strong, tanned fingers were actually going to caress her cheek. Instead they reached forward and gently picked an insect off the sleeve of her blouse.

'You'll be safe here,' Alex promised her softly. 'I'll make sure of it.'

His vow was put to the test earlier than either of them had anticipated. They were back on the road and Lucy kept her eyes glued to the scenery—it was easier that way. Besides, she didn't feel like chatting about inconsequential things. Neither, it seemed, did Alex.

He had just informed her that they were only a couple of miles from his home when a car travelling in the opposite direction took a bend too fast and veered towards them, kicking up dust and grit as its wheels skidded on the sharply curving track.

It all happened so quickly, and yet everything seemed to take place in slow motion too. One minute they were driving along normally, the next Alex was manoeuvring the Jaguar frantically in order to avoid the oncoming vehicle.

Lucy closed her eyes tightly, gripping the edge of her seat as the car screeched to an unexpected halt.

She heard Alex mutter a curse. 'Are you all right?'

She opened her eyes and nodded. 'Yes. Just a bit shaken,' she replied breathlessly. 'For a moment . . .' she gulped a breath ' . . . I . . . I thought we were going to go off the edge.' She glanced sideways and peered out of the window. Just a few feet from where she was sitting, the track disappeared and a sheer drop of thick trees and shrubs took its place.

'Don't look.' Alex's smile was deliberately relaxed. 'It will give you nightmares.'

She glanced behind through the rear window. 'Whoever it was didn't stop,' she murmured. 'Were they from around here, do you suppose?'

'No.' He looked past Lucy towards the valley below. The track was like a winding brown snake. In the distance a trail of dust indicated the car's continued progress. 'Definitely not.' He stared fixedly at the hillside for a moment, intense dark eyes following the vehicle's journey in the distance.

'Did you know the driver?'

Lucy's question seemed to jolt Alex out of his reverie. He looked down at her and frowned. 'What made you ask that?'

She shrugged, a little confused by the stillness of his frame and the sharpness of his question. 'I . . . I don't know,' she murmured. 'It was just your expression . . .'

He released a breath. 'There was something,' he murmured. 'I didn't get a chance to see a great deal, but a flash of hair . . . colours . . . It reminded me of someone . . .' The dark head shook as if he wanted to forget, to shake the image forcibly out of his head. Impatient fingers turned the key in the ignition. 'Let's try and put it out of our minds. Another five minutes and we'll arrive.'

*   *   *

His villa was the sort of home that Lucy dreamed about: comfortable furniture, fine paintings, expensive books, pleasant, interesting objects practically everywhere she looked.

She thought about the cheap bedsitter that she had shared with Paul, with its worn carpet and sad furniture, and had to work hard to repress a shudder.

'You don't look too good.' Dark eyes were surveying her face with a frown.

Lucy inhaled. 'I'm just a little tired, that's all,' she murmured. 'And the trouble with the car…it shook me.'

'I'll show you to your room. You can freshen up and then rest. I have some work I have to do so you'll be left in peace.'

He led her up a narrow staircase, along a passageway that had colourful rugs pinned to the stone walls, past several closed doors, to a large, airy room which overlooked the valley below.

'Oh, this is lovely!' Lucy's smile was genuine as she glanced around, her green eyes sparkling with pleasure at the white walls, the polished furniture, the books and fresh flowers that filled almost every available surface. 'It's just the sort of bedroom I've always wanted!'

'And now you have it—for a short time at least.' Alex placed the cases on the floor at the foot of the four-poster bed. He looked around, as if seeing the room for the first time. 'I asked Maria, the woman from the village, to make sure that it was welcoming, and it seems she's done a good job.'

'It's marvellous, thank you.' Lucy crossed to the window and gazed out across the valley. Her eyes alighted on the aquamarine of the pool shimmering in the afternoon sun. 'It looks very inviting,' she murmured. 'I haven't been swimming in ages.'

'You must swim every day whilst you are here.' He came and stood beside her and once again she felt the sudden, strong, uncompromising presence—an animal magnetism that had unnerved her before whilst travelling with him in the car and was unnerving her again.

'You have a wonderful home.' She moved slightly to put more space between them. He noticed but she couldn't help that. She had never been very relaxed with men—look at how she had been with Paul...

'Yes. I like it. You've had a difficult few months,' Alex continued smoothly. 'You really need to make the most of your time here.'

Lucy ventured the question which had been plaguing her since the beginning. 'You're allowing me to stay here as a favour to Charles. Why is that?' she asked.

Dark eyes surveyed her face impassively. 'Does there have to be a reason?'

'In my experience, people rarely do something for nothing,' she murmured.

'But your experience hasn't been very good, has it?' Alex remarked quietly.

She stared hard at the swimming pool. 'So you do know more than the basic details!' she accused him. 'What exactly has Charles been saying?'

'I told you,' he replied. 'I know about your husband's death. Nothing more. I didn't ask for details.'

'But he gave them to you all the same!' Lucy shook her head angrily. 'Damn Charles!' she murmured quietly. 'He always was a terrible gossip.'

'He cares about you. Surely you know that?'

'Yes.' She pressed her trembling lips together. 'Yes, I know.'

'You look exhausted,' Alex said quietly. 'You need to rest.'

'Don't treat me like a child!' She spun away from the caring voice and concerned eyes and erected a wall of hostility to hide behind. 'I've been married. I've been widowed. I'm a grown woman, for heaven's sake!'

'At the present moment you barely look fifteen,' Alex commented, seemingly unaffected by her sharp outburst. 'If I ask exactly how old you are, will I get my head bitten off again?'

'Most probably!' Lucy kept her gaze fixed on the valley. 'I'm surprised Charles hasn't told you that already. Twenty,' she added, after a few seconds had passed. She glanced across at the far too attractive face and asked pointedly, 'How old are you?'

'A lot older.'

'And wiser no doubt!'

'In some fields, yes.'

'Not all? My, my, you do surprise me! Such modesty.'

She was being a pain again—unnecessarily irritable, just because she was feeling unsure of herself. Just because standing in the same room as this man made her feel weirdly unsettled, excited, confused and totally mixed up.

'I've never been married,' he replied, with brutal smoothness. 'You have the lead on me there.'

'Or widowed?' Lucy's expression was hard. She'd show him.

'No.'

'I disappointed him,' she murmured, fixing her gaze on the view from the window.

'Who? Your husband?'

Lucy's smile was twisted with irony. She shook her head and worked hard at blotting out Paul's deceptively mild countenance. 'No, not my husband. I mean Charles.' She heaved a sigh. 'My behaviour over the last few years...it's not been the best. I was a difficult teenager and then, of course...' there was a telling pause '...I got married. That only reinforced his belief that I was incapable of running my own life in a satisfactory manner. Charles had hoped for great things...'

'And you? Did you hope for great things?'

His question surprised her. She looked across at him and frowned. 'Maybe, at one time...' Lucy thought back to her days at drama school. She had been keen and ambitious then. She nodded, almost reluctantly. 'Yes, I did.'

He looked at her in silence for what seemed like an age, his eyes somehow mesmerising her so that she didn't have the strength to look away. His expression—cool, impassive, almost distant—gave no clues as to what he was thinking. It was unnerving and Lucy didn't know how to handle it.

'You're young,' he asserted firmly. 'You've got a future.'

'You think so?' Alex Darcy had a disconcerting way with him, Lucy decided. He wasn't overly sympathetic, he wasn't particularly friendly, yet she suddenly had an overwhelming need to unburden herself, to tell him things that she had spoken about with no one else. 'At times...' She swallowed, fixing her gaze on the sunlit greenery of the terraces. 'At times,' she repeated slowly, 'I feel ancient inside, like an old, old woman.'

There was a silence. It lengthened to embarrassing proportions. Oh, goodness! Lucy thought wearily. What did I have to tell him that for? If he says something kind now, she told herself, I'll cry; I know I will.

Maybe he read her mind, for there was no trace of compassion or sympathy in his tone when he next spoke. 'We all feel old on occasions,' he replied crisply. 'Life has a habit of wearing even the most resilient down—weakening the strongest.'

'Not you.'

'Why not me?' Alex shook his head, dark eyes smouldering like hot coals in his face. 'You'd be surprised.'

'Would I?' Lucy frowned. 'Tell me, then,' she added firmly. 'When have you not been able to cope?'

'Plenty of times.' His voice was terse, his reply abrupt. It was clear that he wasn't interested in elaborating. 'Take a shower,' he added smoothly. 'There's a bathroom through that door there.' He crossed the room and opened the door, turning to look back at Lucy, who was

still standing before the window, wondering about him.
'Then I think it would be a good idea if you got some
sleep. I'll wake you when it's time for dinner.'

'I'm not feeling particularly hungry,' she murmured.

'Dinner.' Alex repeated firmly. 'See you later.'

Late afternoon had merged with evening. Lucy sat up
on the large four-poster bed and hugged the towelling
robe that she had slipped on after her shower around
her body. Her sleep had been deep and surprisingly refreshing and she felt a whole lot better. Not exactly a
new person, but a vastly improved one.

It was so peaceful. She gazed across at the window
and took a deep breath. The stillness was quite beautiful
after the hustle and bustle of the airport and the warmth
of the car journey.

She wondered what the time was. Early or late? She
couldn't judge by the light in these new surroundings—
not yet, anyway.

After a few moments of just lounging on the bed enjoying the peace, she swung her legs to the floor and
strolled to the open window, breathing in the sweet, warm
air which smelt of citrus fruits and roses. To call this
place your own must be a wonderful thing, she thought.
Absolutely magical.

The bedsit that she had shared with Paul during their
short marriage came into her mind. She had done her
best, but there was no denying that it had been a dump.
Maybe if she had accepted Charles's offer of the down
payment on a flat as a wedding present things would
have worked out, but Lucy had refused and they hadn't.
Stubbornness had always been her weak point. Paul had
been keen, though—too keen; she should have noticed
that. Maybe it would have given her a clue as to what
he was really like. Maybe he had always wanted something for nothing . . .

The silence seemed endless. Too easy to think here, with all this quiet, and thinking was something that she had promised herself she would not do.

Lucy turned away from the window. Where was Alex? Hadn't he said he'd wake her in time for dinner? She listened. The house was quiet. No movement, no rattle of dishes from the kitchen below. Too quiet, maybe?

She walked to the bedroom door and opened it. The thought struck her that she might be alone, and a sudden, unexplained rush of anxiety flooded through her.

'Alex!' Her voice sounded thin and unnatural, echoing against the whitewashed walls. She tried again, her heart sinking when there was no response.

Perhaps something dreadful had happened. Once upon a time she had been like everyone else, imagining that nothing bad would ever touch her. Then she had married Paul and she had seen the stupidity of such naïve assumptions.

Lucy heaved a steadying breath. She was being silly and she knew it. Calm down! she told herself. Go and find your reluctant host; he'll be here somewhere.

She started off at a steady pace, walking briskly but calmly along the passageway, hugging her robe around her as she descended the stairs.

The kitchen was empty. The clock on the wall told her that it was almost nine o'clock, and there was no sign of dinner. No sign of anything or anyone.

'Alex!' Her voice was stronger now, but the response was still the same. Silence.

She ran outside. The heat had subsided and it was a beautiful evening. Orange trees glowed in the dusk, laden with ripe, juicy fruit. Lucy brushed by them unseeing, scanning the terraces, hurrying down the steps to the pool, discovering around a corner a walled vegetable garden that was as beautiful and as deserted as the rest of the place.

Stirrings of panic were starting to take a real hold. Desertion, mugging, death—every possibility ran through her mind. Where was Alex Darcy? How could he do this to her?

She ran back towards the house. Her feet were bare and she cried out in pain as she stepped on a sharp stone and fell forward, sprawling on the sitting area close to the house, where bright geraniums grew in terracotta pots and orange trees shaded the terrace.

'What on earth are you doing?'

She saw his feet first, clad in well-worn loafers; then Alex crouched down and she saw more of him: his legs, tanned and muscular, dusted with a covering of curly black hair; his strong hands resting on his knees; well-worn navy shorts; his broad chest straining against the cotton material of his polo shirt.

'I...I thought you'd gone,' Lucy murmured unsteadily, cursing her foolishness. She scrambled to her feet.

'Gone?' He helped her up, putting one hand around her waist, the other under her arm for support. 'Where would I have gone?'

She swallowed, suddenly breathless. She wasn't sure if it was due to the physical exertions of her search, or relief, or because Alex Darcy was close, holding her with an ease and familiarity that was disturbing and exhilarating all at the same time. She glanced swiftly up into his face, met the stunning eyes and handsome, angular features and looked away again. 'I don't know,' she admitted. 'But the house was so quiet, and when I saw the time...' She shook her head, feeling inadequate under the dark, piercing gaze. 'I thought you'd be in the kitchen, getting dinner,' she mumbled. 'But there was no one there.'

'Is it that late?'

'Nine o'clock.' Lucy looked briefly across to where the sun, blazing like an orange ball, was slipping steadily below the horizon. 'I slept for five hours.'

'Sorry. I tend to forget the time. Whole days slip by without me being aware of it.' The attractive mouth curled. 'It's OK; I'm not a closet alcoholic,' he added with a smile. 'I've been locked away in my study working. Are you very hungry?'

'Yes,' Lucy admitted quietly. He was still holding her. She could feel the strength of his touch through the thick fabric of her robe—demanding, powerful fingers that showed he thought nothing of holding her, nothing of the effect that such a touch could have. 'But it's all right; I can get something for myself,' she added stiltedly. 'If... if you want to carry on with whatever you were doing. Charles did warn me that you were a workaholic.'

'Did he indeed?' Dark eyes slid over her face in amusement, sparkling momentarily. Lucy felt her stomach give a little jolt of excitement. 'No, don't worry, I've had enough for tonight.' Casually Alex released his hold. 'I should stop. Besides, it wouldn't be very hospitable to ask you to eat alone on your first evening here, would it?'

'I wouldn't mind,' she assured him quickly, anxious to make amends for her juvenile behaviour. 'Now I know that you're... that I'm not alone,' she amended swiftly.

'You thought something might have happened to me? Is that why you looked so panic-stricken?' Alex queried. 'How...' he hesitated, searching for the right word '...sweet. I glanced out of my study window and saw you running hell for leather across the terrace—I had no idea such frantic activity was on my account.'

'I called your name and you didn't answer,' Lucy retorted sharply, annoyed by his amusement. 'Anything could have happened.'

'Anything?' The firm mouth curved a little more. 'What had you in mind?'

'Oh, I don't know!' She shook her head, irritated with herself for revealing another of her weaknesses. 'I suffer from a vivid imagination, that's all!'

'Instant pictures, instant panic?'

Lucy nodded reluctantly. 'Yes, that sort of thing. It can make things difficult at times.' She swallowed and felt the lump in her throat.

'It maybe contributed to your. . . illness?'

She hadn't expected him to bring that up so openly. Emerald eyes flashed in defensive anger. 'You mean my *breakdown*?' she queried defiantly. 'You can come right out and say the word, you know,' she added fiercely. 'It won't bite!'

'Yes.' She saw a hint of steel in his eyes. 'Your breakdown.'

'I. . . I don't want to talk about it!' she flared angrily, aware of the contradiction. 'I don't even want to think about it!'

'I wasn't aware I had suggested you do either,' Alex drawled with infuriating smoothness. 'Although, of course, if you feel you want to talk—'

'I won't!'

'You're sure about that?' Stunning eyes disrupted Lucy's rigid expression. 'I'm here. I'm willing to listen.'

'No!' Fear sharpened her voice. 'Of course I don't! You think I would want to dwell on my own failings? To talk about intimate, personal things with you?'

'It crossed my mind. Unburdening yourself can be a great relief. No one can be strong all the time.'

'What would you know about it?' Lucy looked up at him scornfully. She was hiding behind anger again. She hadn't meant the conversation to take this turn. She hadn't expected him to be so open, so. . . forthright.

'Forget dinner!' she replied. 'I'll get myself a sandwich. You go back to your work.'

Strong, tormenting hands took hold of Lucy's arm, preventing her from rushing past. 'Don't tell me what to do in my own home!' It was said with absolute calm, but there was an unmistakable inflexion of steel in the deep voice.

Lucy looked up into the ruggedly attractive face and tried to calm the thudding of her pulse.

'Perhaps now is the time to get one thing straight,' Alex continued crisply. 'I expect a degree of courtesy whilst you are a guest here. I realise you have had a rough time, but that doesn't mean I will tolerate bad manners.'

Lucy's green eyes widened in shock. She was about to reply, but he continued before she could even open her mouth.

'You've been treated with kid gloves by Charles, by the staff at the hospital. That was understandable in the early days, but you cannot expect that sort of treatment indefinitely—'

'I don't!' It was humiliating being spoken to like this. Lucy wished that the patio would open up and swallow her whole. 'It's just—'

'I don't want excuses, or even reasons,' Alex continued with infuriating ease. 'I'm just stating the way things should be from now on. I want you to have a pleasant stay here. I want our relationship to be civilised—'

'Civilised!'

A dark brow rose in query. 'You don't like my choice of word, Lucy?'

'I don't think I like you!' she snapped. 'How dare you patronise me like this? Charles would be so angry if he knew you were speaking to me this way!'

'Charles is not here.'

'I wish he were! I want to leave!'

The attractive mouth curved, but the smile held little amusement. A slight narrowing of the deep, dark eyes showed disapproval. 'Because I dare to question your behaviour?'

'This isn't going to work,' Lucy replied angrily. 'I can't stay here with you! It's a ridiculous idea. I'm going to phone Charles, tell him he has to come and fetch me—' She twisted sharply and found to her amazement that Alex wasn't going to let her go.

'Don't flounce off like a child!'

She glared up at the handsome face. How could this be happening? A few minutes ago she had actually been concerned for this man's welfare! 'I'm not flouncing!' She gulped a steadying breath. 'Would you mind letting go of my arm?' Her voice sounded crisp—so cold that frost was practically dripping off each syllable. Emerald-green eyes clashed with darkest jet, but his hand stayed where it was. 'Didn't you hear what I said?' she asked angrily.

Alex looked at her. 'I heard.'

She moistened her lips. The tension between them was almost tangible. Alex loomed above her, strong and tanned and full of power. She held herself rigid, waiting for the moment to subside. It didn't. The tension became more powerful, subtly changing—an electrical tension that didn't have its roots in anything so straightforward as dislike or hostility.

The strange, almost dangerous silence lengthened. Alex looked down at her. 'You really are a mixed-up young woman, aren't you?' he murmured quietly.

'Quite different from the usual females you *encounter*?'

Lucy put unmistakable emphasis on the last word. She had no idea why she said it—no idea at all. Liar! she told herself. Why can't you admit that what Charles said about Alex Darcy has been on your mind from the first moment you laid eyes on him?

'For ''encounter'' I should presumably read ''meet in bed'',' he replied smoothly. There was another tense silence. 'Has Charles been talking?' Alex drawled dangerously. 'Maybe you're right; maybe he is a terrible old gossip after all. I shall have to have a word with him about it.'

'He was only trying to reassure me!' Lucy answered swiftly, suddenly concerned for her stepbrother's welfare; Alex was big and powerful, whereas Charles was a definite weed. 'He wasn't gossiping at all.'

Alex Darcy looked puzzled—as well he might, she thought miserably; she was getting everything into a terrible tangle.

'Reassure you? What would he need to reassure you about?'

'Oh...you know!'

'Actually I don't; that's why I'm asking,' Alex replied with deceptive mildness. 'Care to explain?'

'Six-foot blondes, with hair the colour of corn!' Lucy muttered.

'*What?*' He wasn't angry; in fact he looked vaguely amused.

She tilted her chin and looked up at him. 'Your regular type of encounter—your women.'

Dark eyes narrowed dangerously. Now he was angry. She had gone too far. Lucy felt a charge of panic.

'Are you deliberately trying to provoke me?'

'N-no.'

'Charles has given you the impression I'm woman-mad—' Alex frowned in noticeable irritation '—is that it?'

'No!' Lucy put a hand to her head. 'I don't know!' she added almost wildly. 'I don't care if you have hundreds of women. It's none of my business, is it?'

'No! Damned right, it's not!'

'Will you let go of my arm now?' she asked shakily. 'I'd...I'd like to go inside.'

'To do what? Pack?'

'To phone Charles, to ask him if he'll come out and fetch me.'

'You know he's busy in Geneva. Besides, if you want to leave that badly you can always book a flight out of here yourself. You're not a prisoner.'

'I haven't got enough money!' Lucy murmured, conscious of the strong fingers still gripping the sleeve of her robe. 'I'm sure Charles has told you that Paul squandered every penny I had earned and saved before he died!'

The coal-black eyes narrowed perceptively. 'No, he didn't.'

'Oh...' Lucy bent her head and looked at the ground. 'Well...he did, and I refused the money Charles offered to tide me over until I can get a job.'

'Why did you do that?'

'Because I don't like charity, that's why!' Lucy flashed. 'Now if you don't mind—'

'What did you do?'

The change of tack disconcerted her for a moment. 'You mean work?' she queried. 'Oh, nothing much. You wouldn't be interested.'

'How do you know? Try me.'

She stared down at the ground self-consciously. 'I...I went to drama school for a while. Then I got work in an office. Nothing very spectacular. I'm not good at anything in particular.'

'Don't undersell yourself!' It was another of what Lucy suspected would turn out to be a long line of rebukes.

She pursed her lips and took a deep breath, staring up into Alex Darcy's face. 'I'm not underselling myself,' she replied frostily. 'Just stating the obvious. Now would you mind letting go of my arm, please? I'd like to go inside to phone Charles.'

'You are a stubborn young woman; you know that, I presume?'

There was a hint of exasperation in his tone. Lucy looked up into the angular face. 'It's been my downfall,' she asserted quietly. 'I realise that now.'

'Well, if you can see that,' Alex replied, without any signs of sympathy, 'surely you'll understand that flouncing out of here after only a few hours is not the most sensible thing to do?'

'You don't want me here,' Lucy murmured. 'That's as plain as day. I don't want to spend time where I'm not wanted.'

'Now you're feeling sorry for yourself!' Alex replied crisply. 'Always a big mistake.'

'Like my stay here!'

The long, lean fingers shook Lucy's arm a little; a mixture of impatience and irritation crossed the handsome face. 'I can't deny Charles's request for help did come out of the blue,' Alex responded sharply, 'but I agreed to have you here and I stand by that arrangement.'

Her green eyes narrowed provokingly. 'You're regretting it, though, aren't you?'

His sensuous lips compressed into a firm line and his fingers pulled her closer towards the large, broad frame. 'Will you stop forcing the point, Lucy? You're being totally impossible.' He surveyed her with an irritated gaze. 'I live a solitary life—always have, always will. I can't deny that your presence here will take a bit of getting used to, but I'm perfectly capable of being sociable if you'll act in an appropriate manner.'

She frowned up at him. 'And what do you mean by that?'

'If you'll stop acting like a petulant child!'

'Maybe I want to act like a petulant child; maybe I always have!' She didn't care what he thought of her. She didn't! For the past few weeks she hadn't cared about anything much at all. Lucy tried to shake his hand free, but his grip was firm and uncompromising, matching his expression. 'Will you let go of me?' she gritted.

'No.'

She had an overwhelming desire to stamp her bare feet on the dusty ground, to pull and tug herself free and run off sobbing. 'I want you to!' she told him wildly.

'No, you don't.' His voice was calm and controlled. 'Tell me something.'

'What?' Lucy tilted her chin and eyed Alex warily. He looked so handsome, so completely male—cool and totally in command.

'When was the last time you here held?'

Her heart skipped a beat. 'I...I don't know.' She shook her head, hardly daring to meet his gaze, repeating the word as if she hardly knew its meaning. *'Held?'*

'Yesterday?' Alex persisted. 'A week ago, a month?'

Lucy stared up at the smouldering eyes and felt every nerve-end tingling as a new, quite daunting prospect loomed into view. 'I...I can't remember,' she murmured evasively.

'I shouldn't imagine Charles is particularly good at hugging, is he?' Alex continued smoothly. 'And there's no one else now, is there?' He released a breath and the firm line of his mouth softened a little as he looked at Lucy. 'You lose someone—someone close—and everyone backs off. They don't mean to, but grief is difficult to deal with. Even the simplest phrases of condolence sound clichéd or banal, don't they?'

'Yes.' She contemplated the strong, rugged planes of his face and nodded slowly, remembering, marvelling at the fact that he actually understood how it had been. 'Yes, they do.'

'Your friends probably did their best, but it's not always good enough, is it?'

Lucy released a tense breath. She was inches away from him, and the proximity of such blatant animal magnetism coupled with this sudden unexpected sensitivity was not helping her to stay aloof and unmoved.

'I...I haven't many friends. Not any more. Paul...' She faltered, gulping a swift breath. 'He...he didn't get on with them,' she finished reluctantly.

'He could be a difficult man?'

Strain clenched her features; her throat ached with unshed tears. Never speak ill of the dead. It wasn't right to criticise Paul now, especially not with a stranger. 'He was my husband,' she murmured unsteadily.

'And you loved him.' It was said as if that fact were a forgone conclusion.

Lucy didn't bother to contradict him. It was what everyone thought, she knew that. After all, they had only been married a couple of months and she had grieved so after his death. Grieved for all the wrong reasons...but grieved nonetheless.

'I'm sorry if I was harsh earlier,' Alex murmured. 'I apologise.'

'I deserved it,' Lucy muttered awkwardly. 'But apology accepted anyway.' She gulped a breath, conscious of the tears that were threatening to overwhelm her. When people were kind, she cried—it was an equation that she didn't know how to overcome.

'It's OK,' Alex murmured gently, brushing a finger across her damp cheek. 'Tears don't frighten me. You don't have to feel embarrassed.'

'I don't *want* to cry!' She hung her head as she fought to prevent her tears. 'I'm sick of feeling miserable, of being an object of pity.'

'Self-pity?'

Lucy looked up. He could be remarkably brutal when it suited him. 'Maybe,' she whispered.

'Honesty.' A half-smile twisted the corners of his mouth. 'I approve. Don't be too hard on yourself,' he added firmly. 'No one's perfect.'

'Not even you?' Her attempt at lightness almost killed her, but she felt proud that she had managed it when she saw his smile.

'Not even me.'

She couldn't reply. Another light-hearted retort would have been the best, the safest approach then—something flippant to defuse the tension in the far too personal nature of their conversation. But she knew it would be impossible. She recognised brooding compassion in Alex's expression and swallowed back the lump in her throat. 'Don't!' she croaked, shaking her head. 'Please—!'

He took no notice. Deep down, Lucy knew, she hadn't wanted him to.

Alex pulled her towards his solid frame, and the tears that she had held back for so long streamed like a torrent down her pale cheeks.

CHAPTER TWO

Lucy had expected a quick hug, had counted on being released after a few short seconds. But the holding just went on and on.

She wanted it to; that was the shocking thing. The fact that she craved the feeling of the firm, male body pressed so effectively against her own stunned her absolutely. Never before had she experienced such an overwhelming need to be held, to keep on being held—never with her husband, that much was certain.

The grieving widow. It indicated so much and yet revealed so little. Lucy closed her eyes and gripped Alex's shirt tightly.

'Are you OK?'

His voice was deep and husky and that made it worse—more difficult to disentangle herself. She felt weak with confusion. How could she feel this much physical awareness of a man she didn't know and certainly didn't much like?

'Lucy?' Insistent hands slackened her hold. Alex leaned back and tried to look into her face. 'Will you look at me?'

'No!' She didn't want to see that gaze. Too dark and attractive, too perceptive, he would recognise and understand the sexual attraction which had sprung out of nowhere and had to be repressed at all costs.

Lucy had felt guilty enough before; for weeks before Paul's death she had been wishing that her marriage would end, that he would exit her life and leave her in peace, but now she felt even worse.

A widow of less than two months and already wanting another man.

Any man? she wondered miserably. Or just this one?

'Don't touch me!' Lucy found the strength she needed from somewhere and tugged fiercely. Immediately she found herself released. 'What do you think you're trying to do?' she cried. 'Make me go mad?' She wiped the tears from her face with the back of her hand and then, half stumbling away from him, ran into the house.

Let him think her crazed and deranged, she thought. What did she care? She knew better than anyone what a mixed-up young woman she was. She just couldn't cope with Alex Darcy mixing her up any more.

He followed her, and she knew instinctively that that spelt trouble. Confrontations clearly didn't frighten the life out of him the way they did her. She turned and faced him in the hallway of the house, conscious of herself, of him, of the cool interior and the deathly silence that enveloped them both as they looked at one another.

'Just leave me alone!' Lucy muttered unsteadily. 'Stop pestering me!'

'Pester—?' Incredulous exasperation crossed Alex's face. 'What on earth are you talking about?'

'Harassing me, then!' Lucy amended hurriedly, conscious that she was only making things worse as he drew in a dangerous breath and took a step towards her. 'Oh, I don't know!' she added almost wildly. 'But, whatever it is, stop doing it!'

'I held you because you needed comfort,' Alex replied crisply. 'You seemed glad of it at the time.'

'You seem to imagine too much!' Lucy flashed. 'I was confused, that's all. I wasn't thinking straight. Maybe I do need someone to hold me, but not you! Never someone like you!'

'Someone like me?' She saw the line of his jaw harden, the dark eyes narrow as he repeated her words. 'What are you talking about?' He walked towards her. No menace in his steps, just an irrepressible intent. 'Lucy, calm down! Working yourself up like this is not the right thing to do, believe me.'

'I . . . I'm not worked up,' Lucy asserted weakly, conscious as she took a faltering step backwards of the roughness of the stone wall behind her. 'You can't do this to me!'

Dark brows were raised quizzically. 'Do what?' he enquired, frowning. 'What is it I can't do?'

'You know,' Lucy whispered, watching as jet-black eyes lingered on her face. 'You know very well.'

'No, Lucy, I don't.' He shook his head slowly, looking at her with eyes that held humiliating puzzlement. Then his expression cleared and he added softly, 'It was just a platonic hug. Nothing to worry about.'

'I know, I know!' Lucy's denial was a fraction too swift, a fraction too unsteady.

'But you wanted it to be something more? Is that what's worrying you? Look, it's nothing to be ashamed about,' Alex insisted smoothly, watching Lucy's rigid face. 'We all have different needs, different ways of coping. You shouldn't feel guilty about the way your body reacts. Is that why you pulled away and fled like a scared rabbit?' He reached out and touched her cheek with the palm of his hand. 'Is it?'

'You are so arrogant!' Lucy snapped, jerking away from his touch. 'What makes you think I would ever want to—?'

'I was talking hypothetically,' Alex cut in sharply. 'Sexual needs don't always vanish into thin air because a partner dies. You still want your husband, you miss the physical side of your relationship; it happens.'

Lucy muttered an incoherent curse beneath her breath. He didn't understand. He thought like all the rest—that she still yearned for Paul, still wanted him here beside her. The truth was that Paul had been the furthest thing from her mind when Alex had held her. 'You sound like a psychiatrist!' Lucy murmured unsteadily. 'Thank you, but I had more than enough analysis at the hospital!'

'Lucy!' Something in his tone made her take notice. She glanced across and frowned. 'What?'

Alex didn't speak immediately. Lucy saw a flicker of indecision cross the angular features and wondered whether he was about to tell her that maybe she should leave, that it probably was for the best that they called a halt to the arrangement here and now. 'I'm not the sort of man who plays games; you need have no fear of that.'

Lucy kept her gaze as steady as she could. 'I'm pleased to hear it.'

More hesitation. More intrigue. There was something he seemed to want to say—something difficult maybe... 'I know what it's like to lose someone you love.' Dark eyes held hers with magnetic force and Lucy knew that she couldn't look away even if she wanted to. 'Charles sent you here because he trusts me,' Alex continued, in deep, vibrant tones. 'I want you to trust me, too.'

'I'm not very good at trusting people,' Lucy replied stiffly. 'I trusted Paul and—' She halted abruptly, conscious that she had a need to confide again.

'And what?'

'Please!' She shook her head and stared up at Alex imploringly. 'I really don't want to talk about it.'

'I'm pushing too hard.' He smiled—a warm, relaxed curve of his mouth that sent Lucy's pulse racing all over again. 'Sorry.'

She had a choice: keep it polite and cool, so that Alex was left in no doubt about how she wanted things to proceed, or try and make an effort, show him that underneath the panic she could respond like a perfectly sane and happy human being.

'Again?' she murmured. There was a hint of a smile, a slight lifting of an eyebrow. It had been the right choice; somehow the tension melted away.

''Fraid so.' Dark eyes sparkled magnetically, and Lucy found her smile widening, despite everything that had gone before. 'That's better. You know...that smile...' Alex raised a hand, as if to touch the very thing which he was talking about, and Lucy held her breath, watching his compelling face in fascination, her emerald eyes glued to the taut, dynamic features.

The tension was back, or had it never gone away? Would he touch her mouth? *Would he?*

It seemed not. A firm line replaced the smile; the stunning eyes grew dark and daunting. Alex lowered his hand suddenly and turned away. 'I'll make a start on dinner!' he informed her with crisp precision. He walked away towards the kitchen. 'Why don't you go upstairs and get changed?'

'I could help.' Lucy followed him through the stone archway and down the steps, watching as he opened cupboards and drawers with angry, jerky movements.

'It's OK.'

'But I don't mind, honestly! It will be nice for me to *do* something constructive for a change—'

'Didn't you hear what I said?' Alex turned and faced Lucy and there was brutal impatience in his expression. 'I don't need your help.' He breathed in and Lucy saw the effort he needed to school his features into milder lines. 'Honestly. This is your first night here, so I'll do the work. Maybe tomorrow. How about that?'

'There's no need to speak to me as if I'm a child.' Lucy's voice was quiet but full of intensity. 'I'll go upstairs,' she added swiftly, forestalling any reply. 'As you ordered.'

The loggia—a wonderful open-sided balcony that in daytime afforded breathtaking views of the lush green hills and the distant, sparkling blue sea beyond—was the sort of place you saw in glossy magazines.

It was still very warm, despite the lateness of the hour. Lucy took some salad from the bowl that Alex was holding out to her and busied herself with arranging the crisp green leaves on her plate.

He looked even more sensational than before. He had showered and changed since preparing dinner and now he was wearing a pristine white shirt and cream trousers which emphasised the deepness of his tan and the glossy darkness of his hair.

'So, how do you plan to spend tomorrow?' he asked.

Lucy tried to keep her voice suitably neutral. 'Oh, just lazing around, I suppose.' She deliberately avoided eye contact, concentrating instead on buttering a crusty roll. 'A walk, perhaps; a dip in the pool—if it's all right with you, of course,' she added hurriedly.

'Fine. Do whatever you wish,' Alex replied evenly. 'You have the run of the place whilst you're here, so you may as well make the most of it.'

'Thank you.'

'My pleasure.'

Lucy got the impression that he was laughing at her, although when she risked a glance his gaze was perfectly impassive. Their eyes met and Lucy looked down hurriedly. She felt dreadfully self-conscious under Alex Darcy's vibrant eyes—uncertain, unsure of herself in relation to him.

After months of not caring how she looked, she had this evening found the inclination to arrange her long auburn tresses into a more sophisticated style, tying her long, fiery hair with a bright yellow silk scarf so that it fell in thick waves over one shoulder. Lucy adjusted the strap of her sundress self-consciously. It was a plain garment, but the simple lines suited her slender figure, and the pale lemon of the fabric contrasted well with the richness of her hair and the sudden glow that was rising up from her throat to cover her face.

Had Alex noticed that she had made an effort with her appearance? Did he like what he saw? She watched as his gaze briefly scanned her body, but he didn't say anything, so she supposed not.

Lucy gave an inward sigh. She felt disappointed, and that was ridiculous. Common sense told her that Alex Darcy was used to far more stunning sights than she. Just because she had spent over an hour getting ready...

'You can look upon tomorrow as a fresh start,' Alex declared. 'Believe me, this place has incredible healing powers. You'll wake up tomorrow morning with the warmth of the sun on your face, wander outside onto the terrace, pick fresh oranges for your breakfast... I guarantee you'll feel like a new woman in no time.'

'I hope so.' Lucy took a sip of chilled mineral water and concentrated purposefully on the darkened view. 'I'm not particularly keen on holding onto the old one.' There was an awkward pause. 'Warm sun will be a real change,' she added, frantically trying to keep the conversation upbeat, 'after the weather we've been having in England—it's been one of the coldest springs on record.'

Dark brows were raised sardonically. 'Again?'

'Did you leave England to escape the weather?' Lucy ventured, unable to deny her sudden interest in the man opposite her.

The tone of his voice changed; it became wooden, slightly edgy. He picked up a fork and speared some food. 'It was one of the reasons.'

There were others, clearly. Lucy wondered what they were, but something about Alex's demeanour told her that further enquiry would not be particularly welcome, and she wasn't sure that she had the nerve to pursue it. 'Charles mentioned you haven't returned in a long while. Don't you miss the old country?' she enquired lightly.

'No.' Alex held Lucy's gaze without flinching. 'Why? Should I?'

His expression was suddenly harder, almost cold. 'No... no, of course not.' There was to be no discussion at all about England; that much was clear. Lucy glanced down at her plate to avoid the formidable chill that had appeared in Alex's eyes. 'I just thought that—'

'I have no reason to return, no ties that bind me.' Alex glanced around the loggia, then turned in his chair to look at the view behind. 'This is my home now.'

'You have no family?' Lucy queried hesitantly.

'No. My parents died a few years ago.' There was a significant pause. 'I will be working all day tomorrow,' he continued, handing a bowl of succulent-looking pasta to Lucy, precluding, with the sudden change of subject, any more obviously unacceptable enquiries of a personal nature. 'In my study. That is the only place I would prefer you not to enter whilst you are a guest here. I have a deadline I must meet, so if I don't emerge until dusk, or even beyond, don't worry.' His mouth twisted in sudden amusement. 'I'll still be alive.'

So, he doesn't like personal talk, Lucy mused. She wondered why not. Did Alex Darcy have parts of his life that he preferred not to talk or even think about? Was there pain in his past too? It was an intriguing thought.

'Charles mentioned that you are a writer,' Lucy murmured, after several seconds had passed. She forked the moist tagliatelle into her mouth and found that for the first time in weeks she actually wanted to go on eating. 'It sounds exciting.'

Safer ground now. Lucy looked across into the handsome face and saw that the smouldering tension had eased a little. 'Hardly that,' Alex replied drily. 'Satisfying, though, when things go well.'

'But you're successful, aren't you?' Lucy insisted. 'Some of your books have been turned into films. I'm not a great reader, but I can remember Charles getting all excited a couple of years ago because a friend of his was short-listed for the Booker Prize—that was you, wasn't it?'

'You astonish me.' Alex looked at Lucy with mild surprise. 'I didn't think Charles held my writing career in particularly high regard.'

'Oh, he does!' Lucy replied. 'He's not the dry old stick that everyone assumes he is! Do you hope to repeat your success?'

Alex lifted his shoulders in a shrug and proceeded to tuck into his plateful of food with healthy enthusiasm. 'Always hoping. But who can tell? I'm working on it.'

Lucy glanced across with interest. She hadn't had a conversation that didn't seem to link up with her own predicament in a long while and it felt wonderfully refreshing to take an interest in somebody else's affairs for a change. 'Where do you get your ideas from?'

Alex waved a negligent hand. Lucy sensed that he wasn't particularly interested in the subject, or maybe his lack of enthusiasm came about because it was a subject that he had discussed so many times with so many people. His friends. Who were they? What were they like? Suddenly Lucy found herself wanting to know.

'Oh, in the shower, when I'm out walking, watching a sunset...eating a meal...' He flashed a smile and even white teeth gleamed in contrast against the deeply bronzed face. Lucy felt warm, as if the sun had deigned to shine upon her. 'The oddest moments.'

'But you like what you do?' she persisted.

'Yes,' Alex admitted. 'It's a creative challenge if nothing else.' There was a slight pause as he contemplated Lucy's interested face, then he added, 'Who am I trying to kid? I love it. I wouldn't want to do anything else. When a story works well, when the book has been published and is selling like hot cakes...well, then it's absolutely exhilarating.'

Lucy stared out towards the hills. 'That's what I need,' she murmured. 'A new venture. Something good and solid that I can work at. To be a success. If there's one thing Charles likes it's success. That's why I'm such a disappointment to him. He would have loved it if I had entered one of the traditional professions—lawyer, doctor, any of those.' Lucy raised another forkful of food to her lips. 'Incidentally, how did you and Charles meet?' she added. 'He usually spends all his time with men in dark grey suits.'

'And you can't see me in one of those?' Ebony eyes glimmered in sudden amusement.

She found her gaze lingering on the firm, muscled chest, the tanned forearms, the strength of neck and shoulders. 'Not at the moment, no.' Lucy returned Alex's smile and found to her amazement that she was beginning to relax. 'Was it through work? It must have been—Charles doesn't believe in play; he says he thrives on being dull and boring.'

'I was on a committee he was chairing,' Alex replied briefly. 'We went for a drink after a particularly gruelling session and found we hit it off. You know, underneath that rigid exterior you have a stepbrother who happens to possess quite a dry sense of humour!'

'Oh, I know! He isn't quite as staid as he looks! I just wish he would let himself go a little more.' Lucy picked up her glass again. 'So Charles was chairman, was he?' she added. 'He revels in all that power; that's why he's a politician, I suppose. Was it to do with the arts?' Lucy thought about it and frowned. 'I don't recall Charles having anything to do with that sort of thing. He's usually involved with far more boring subjects, like finance.'

'It was a long time ago,' Alex replied shortly. 'A part of my life that simply doesn't exist any more. Before my writing career took off,' he added, as if that were sufficient explanation.

'Oh, so you haven't always been a writer, then? I assumed—'

'Dangerous to assume!' Alex cut in swiftly. He flashed her a sensational smile and expertly diverted the conversation. 'Drama school. What was that like? Did you ever get any acting work?'

'A couple of small parts in children's series. Two or three advertisements for television. I got my Equity card, which is something, I suppose.'

'You didn't stick with it?'

'I don't think I had any real talent. My tutors were
quite encouraging, but...' Lucy hesitated. 'I had met
Paul by that time, anyway,' she added briskly.

'So?' Dark brows were raised in query. 'Why should
that stop you? You did want to be an actress, I presume?'

'It didn't stop me.' She realised that her voice had
come out sounding rather strident. She modified her tone
and added, 'Somehow everything seemed to get side-
tracked, that's all. Paul thought I'd be better off going
out and getting a proper job.'

She could feel Alex's eyes upon her, assessing what
she had just said, but she didn't return his gaze. She'd
done it again: revealed herself to him, given him food
for thought—told him more than she'd ever told anyone.
'We wanted to set up home and there were things we
had to buy,' Lucy added hurriedly. 'We needed the
money.'

'Your husband—'

'I don't want to talk about him!'

'I was just going to ask if he had a career,' Alex murmured. 'Don't worry; nothing too personal. I got my
head bitten off once before, remember? I'm not quite
ready to have it bitten off again.'

'I've been a bit of a pain, haven't I?' Lucy murmured.
'Sorry.'

'You've had a hard time.' Alex's tone was crisp and
matter-of-fact. 'It's understandable.'

'Paul didn't like to be tied down to regular work. He
did have a job when I met him,' she added quickly, wondering why she was bothering to say any of this, 'but
after a couple of months he got laid off.'

Lucy risked a glance across the table and saw that Alex
appeared less than interested. Why don't you just come
right out and say he was sacked? she asked herself. Be
honest about it. Paul's dead. You don't have to cover
up for him any more!

'He had more of a hippy attitude, really,' she continued. 'He sort of drifted.' Lucy looked at Alex and

managed at least a modicum of honesty. 'For a while I found myself drifting too.'

She looked at him then, saw the frown, the vague disapproval in his expression. Clearly he didn't like slackers. 'I got a position in an office, but I...I didn't feel too well for a while, and I decided to give it up.'

'Nothing serious, I hope?'

Serious? Lucy lowered her head to her plate and remembered how easy it was to lose her appetite. Was having a baby serious? It was important, she knew that much. Devastating when you lost it, or were made to lose it...

'I hated office work anyway,' she continued hurriedly. 'It was a relief to leave.'

'So, you'll be trying something new? Maybe you'll pick up the pieces of your acting career?'

'I doubt it,' she murmured. 'All that feels as if it happened centuries ago. I'll probably end up in an office again.'

'Are you always so defeatist?'

Lucy looked across, surprised by the sudden vehemence in Alex's voice. 'I'm just being...realistic,' she replied haltingly.

'No, you're not!' He shook his head and threw her a disparaging look. 'You're just taking the easy option. How it annoys me when people settle for second best.' Dark eyes flashed across the table at her. 'Why don't you fight for what you want?' he demanded. 'If you hate the way your life is going, then do something about it!'

'Easy for you to say,' she returned quickly, 'sitting there with a successful career and your independence!'

'They weren't handed to me on a plate,' Alex delivered with cool precision. 'I had to work hard to get where I am. Years of slog in a profession that I ended up hating. Years of rejection slips one after another, with no one believing in me except myself.'

'But you've got talent; you can do something—!'

'And you can't?' Smouldering dark eyes bit into her. 'You're saying you're useless?'

'No! Yes!' She shook her head and felt a wash of desolation sweep over her. 'Oh, I don't know!'

'Well, I suggest you find out!' Alex replied crisply. 'You need to start looking at your life, at what you want to achieve. You can't drift for ever, Lucy. The future has to be faced.'

'I know that! I don't need you to tell me!' she retorted angrily. What on earth had made her think that this man possessed any sort of compassion? She stood up, scraping her chair back from the table, listening to the sound of her cutlery as it fell from her plate to the floor. 'You're so damned sure of yourself!' she exclaimed. 'It makes me sick! I didn't come here to be lectured to; I came here to recuperate!'

'Thinking seriously about your future is part of re-cuperation,' he replied instantly.

She couldn't stand any more. Strain clenched Lucy's delicate features. She glared at Alex Darcy. That man! So damned sure of himself! What did he know? How could he sit there and make such cool statements about her life, about the way she should think? It wasn't fair that he should judge her without knowing the facts.

She met the hard, critical look in his eyes and almost wished for a moment that he did know every detail. But that thought didn't last more than a few seconds. Imagine how much worse his judgement would be, she told herself, if he knew how easily it had been for Paul to manipulate her, how weak she had been with him. Alex Darcy would undoubtedly take the tough line: women who allowed their husbands to treat them like slaves had only themselves to blame, and if it meant losing a baby in the process...a baby that no one outside the marriage knew existed...

Lucy closed her eyes. She couldn't think about all that again. Goodness knew she had spent enough time tor-turing herself already.

At the door to the loggia she turned back briefly to find Alex surveying her with an expression that was difficult to decipher. His observation was disconcerting—so intense suddenly, as if he wanted to look into her very soul.

'If I had known what a self-righteous swine you were,' Lucy declared heatedly, 'I would never have agreed to come!'

'And if I had known about your defeatist attitude and your stubborn streak,' Alex replied in clipped tones, 'then I would have stood my ground and not allowed Charles to persuade me to have you here against my better judgement.'

It had been meant to hurt and it did. Although why so much, Lucy didn't know—after all, she had guessed in that first moment of seeing Alex that he was allowing her to stay at his home on sufferance. Hearing the truth now shouldn't have made that much difference.

'I'll go if that's what you want!' She stared at him bleakly. The evening had been going so well until now. All of a sudden Lucy felt tired again, and worn out, and very, very unhappy.

She heard a muttered curse, looked up with misted eyes and saw that Alex was getting to his feet. 'Of course, it's not!' He threw down his napkin impatiently and strode towards her.

He came near and her mouth quivered tremulously. 'But you said—'

'I know what I said!' His voice was harsh. 'I know what I said,' he repeated more softly. 'Lucy, I—' He dragged strong fingers through his dark hair and shook his head, cursing again, only more softly this time, beneath his breath. 'This is . . . going to be difficult. I had no idea.'

'What?' She looked up, brushing a strand of hair away from her face, and frowned. Alex, she thought, looked almost tortured, as if he badly regretted being horrible to her. 'Me? You mean I'm difficult?'

'Charles certainly doesn't have a clue about you, does he?' Alex released a deep breath, noticed the puzzlement clouding her features and shook his head again. 'It doesn't matter. I'm just thinking out loud. Your devoted stepbrother just didn't prepare me very well, that's all. Maybe you should go to bed.' Alex's voice was rough again. 'You did say you were tired.'

He didn't want her around. She bored him. All her gushing about his work, and her probing into his life, and then her petulant anger. No wonder he could hardly stand the sight of her.

'Charles has put you in a very awkward position, hasn't he?' Lucy murmured. 'I really irritate you beyond belief!'

'Irritation has very little to do with it,' Alex replied drily. 'Believe me.' There was a slight pause. 'Your hair is coming loose,' he murmured. He pulled at the yellow silk bow and held it out to her, watching the auburn strands as they swung free from the restraint of the scarf. 'You have remarkable hair. That was another thing Charles never mentioned.'

'There were others?' She took the scarf from his out-stretched hand, aware of the sudden potency in his gaze. She felt confused. The whole mood of their conversation kept swinging like a pendulum. One minute everything seemed to be OK, the next there were sparks flying.

'Plenty of things.'

Their fingers touched and sexual attraction sliced through her like a knife. Was it mutual, she wondered, or did Alex look at all women like this? She waited, hovering in agonised uncertainty. She should move away, she thought, but something about his gaze, something about the way he made her feel kept her standing there, feet rooted firmly to the spot.

'Alex—'

'Go to bed, Lucy!' The roughness in his voice didn't quite match his expression, but it was enough to make her realise that she had been imagining certain things simply to suit herself. 'You're tired. I'm tired.' Alex's eyes avoided her hurt expression. He moved towards the door. 'We'll both be able to cope better with all this in the morning.'

'All what?' She walked towards him, suddenly defiant.

'Do I have to spell it out?' His glance was brief but telling. 'Neither of us is what the other expected; I think we can both agree on that.'

'You mean I'm far more annoying than you had imagined?' she persisted riskily. 'Is that it?'

'Don't play games!' Alex gritted in a low voice. 'They're not worthy of you. Besides, you'll only end up losing.' Smouldering dark eyes bit into her face. 'We both will. Now get some rest.' Alex held open the door and dared Lucy to disobey with an expression that was as hard as steel. 'I'll see you in the morning.'

Sleep was ages in coming. The bed was fresh and cool, her skin washed and sweet-smelling after a long, hot shower. But the passing hours saw Lucy becoming more and more agitated and uptight as she twisted and turned in the big four-poster bed. She was used to sleepless nights; goodness knew she had endured enough of them since Paul's car accident—hours and hours spent dwelling on his death and their failed marriage, even longer mourning the loss of a baby that had existed for only a few weeks, alive but unseen, growing inside her stomach, a source of annoyance for Paul but of great joy for her...

And now she had Alex Darcy to cope with. Or rather the feelings that his proximity conjured up. He didn't find her very likeable; that much was clear. And she didn't like him. But that, it seemed, didn't stop her being attracted to him physically. When he was near to her, she felt...thrilled, disturbed—like a schoolgirl with a crush on an idol.

Lucy bashed her pillow into shape for the hundredth time, cursing beneath her breath. It didn't make sense. She needed to sleep. She had to stop thinking about him...

It was in here somewhere! Lucy opened another drawer and searched frantically for the baby's shawl. She had washed and ironed and folded it, and now it had disappeared. She banged the drawer shut and opened another one, knocking her shins in the process but feeling no pain. Not here either. *Where was it?* She left the chest of drawers in a state of disarray and walked along the passageway, bumping into a wooden chair with eyes that were open but didn't see.

In the room at the end? She opened the bedroom door and walked in. Moonlight shone on the polished wooden floor, silhouetting Lucy's slender frame, revealing her naked body beneath the flimsy nightgown.

The shawl—she had to find it. Urgency was revealed in her actions now. Doors were slammed, furniture disturbed. A tea chest in the corner of the room was rifled with unseeing eyes. So much to do and so little time in which to do it! The baby was growing cold with every moment that passed. If she didn't find the shawl it would die...

'What the—?' Alex Darcy watched from the doorway. His dark hair was tousled, the line of his jaw heavy with a fresh growth of beard. A hastily tied robe revealed a large expanse of tanned chest. He stood perplexed, observing Lucy, who was busy with an unknown task. She didn't appear to have seen him... and then he saw that she wasn't seeing anything.

She was sleepwalking.

His assessing male gaze rested briefly on the full curve of creamy breast and the taut line of thigh and buttock as she roamed the moonlit room in restless endeavour.

'Lucy.' He spoke her name gently, moving forward into the room. She turned and looked at him, and for a moment he thought that she really did see.

'I'm going to find it!' she announced crisply. 'You've hidden it. You knew I wanted it specially and you've thrown it away!'

'Lucy, I think you should go back to bed. We can find whatever it is you're looking for in the morning.' Alex took another step towards her and held out his hand. 'Come on,' he added soothingly. 'I'll show you the way back to bed.'

'No!' The emerald eyes were wide now with anger. 'No, I won't go with you! I want the shawl. Give it to me!'

Alex frowned. A look of compassion crossed the strong, dark features. 'Lucy, I'm not who you think I am,' he replied evenly. 'You're dreaming. Now come back to bed.'

'No!' Her eyes were wild with hate. 'Where's the shawl? The baby needs it. You have to give it to me!'

Alex stood motionless, considering the best approach. When he spoke his voice was firmer, more commanding. 'Come with me! You need to get back to bed.' He guided her hand into his, holding it gently. 'We'll find the shawl in the morning,' he promised. 'Don't worry about it.'

'But I want it!' she wailed pitifully, pulling her hand out of his, returning to the tea chest. 'The baby will get cold.' She shivered in the moonlight—a tremor that ran the length of her body, all anger gone now. '*I'm* cold!' she murmured. 'You've turned the heating off again!'

'You'll be all right.' Alex gently manoeuvred her away from the jumble of his old possessions and turned her to face him. 'Here, take this.' Alex untied his robe and gently placed it around Lucy's trembling shoulders.

He was naked beside her now, his taut, muscled frame gleaming in the moonlight, but she wasn't in the least aware of his state of undress. Alex's mouth curved slightly as he imagined Lucy's reaction should she choose to wake up at this particular moment.

'Is that better?' he asked gently.

'Yes...yes, I suppose so.'

A thought occurred to him. He hesitated a moment and then asked, 'What's my name?'

Her reply was immediate. 'Paul.'

'Would you like Paul to take you back to your bed?'

'No!' Lucy shook her head and tried to tug her hand free. 'No!'

'Shh!' Alex, startled by the look of dismay on her face, worked hard at keeping his voice calm. 'It's OK. Paul's not here now. He's gone. He won't touch you.'

'He hasn't hidden the shawl?' she queried, her brows drawing together in a frown.

'No.'

'Good.' Her body visibly relaxed. She turned towards Alex and rested her head against his chest. 'Hold me,' she whimpered. 'Please!'

'I'm Alex. Not Paul.'

'Yes,' Lucy said sleepily. 'Alex...'

Her hair was soft and sweet-smelling. He stared down at it, and, after a moment's hesitation, gently placed his arms around Lucy's shoulders. She was calmer now; she would allow herself to be led back to her room without any trouble. He was just about to suggest that very thing when the auburn head twisted around and Lucy looked up.

'Kiss me,' she mumbled sleepily.

'Lucy!' Alex released a tense breath. He closed his eyes and wondered if he himself weren't having some sort of crazy dream. 'Lucy,' he repeated.

'Please!' She tilted her head and pressed her lips enticingly against his. They were so soft—just like the feel of her body. And she was so sweet, so delicate...

Alex lowered his head, cradling her face with his hands. It was so tempting to respond, to move his lips over hers, to gently experience the warmth of her mouth.

She was like a child, but an intensely attractive one. How many years between them? It felt like a lifetime.

If she awoke now, if she realised what was going on...

Slowly and with infinite care Alex did as she asked, his mouth moving sensuously over her lips. He felt her move against him, felt the stir of desire running through his own body as she tightened her hold on his arms and instinctively he responded, deepening the kiss, moving her body closer so that he could feel the firmness of each and every curve...

The strength of his arousal shocked him deeply. This shouldn't be happening. It felt absolutely right, but of course it couldn't be, not like this, not with a girl who had recently experienced so much torment and clearly didn't know her own mind.

Alex pulled away with a groan of regret and anger at his own weakness.

The walk along the landing seemed to last as long as eternity. The four-poster bed gleamed invitingly in the moonlit room and a picture flashed into Alex's mind, of tangled limbs and hot, passionate kisses.

Lucy slipped beneath the sheets, mumbled something incoherent and then closed her eyes.

Alex stood for a moment looking down at the glossy hair and beautiful face. Don't even think about it! he told himself. It would be doomed from start to finish.

The strong mouth hardened into a firm line and Alex picked up his fallen robe and exited the room, working hard at thrusting all thoughts of the nubile young body and careworn face from his mind.

Lucy saw the chest of drawers in disarray and felt the soreness on her shins as she got out of bed, bleary-eyed and without much enthusiasm, next morning.

She stared at her clothes as she searched for a T-shirt and shorts in puzzlement. Why were the drawers in such a mess? Had there been a burglary?

She glanced across the room. It didn't seem likely. Her handbag was resting on the chair where she had left it and she could see that her purse was still inside.

She stripped off her nightdress and headed for the shower, too tired to give it a great deal of attention.

Half an hour later she found Alex in the kitchen, eating fresh pastries and drinking a cup of coffee. He looked the exact opposite of how she felt—fresh and sharp, vitality exuding from every handsome pore.

'Morning.' He looked up from his newspaper and kept on looking as Lucy crossed the kitchen towards the stove, where a large pot of steaming coffee waited invitingly. 'How are you feeling?'

'OK.' She glanced briefly in his direction, vaguely puzzled by something particular in his enquiry. 'You?'

'Fine.' He folded up the paper and leant back in his chair, watching, Lucy felt, with an unexplainable curiosity. 'Did you sleep well?'

She hesitated. She poured black coffee into a colourful pottery mug and thought about the agonies of last night. 'Eventually,' she murmured. 'I could have done with a couple of sleeping pills.'

'You're better off without them,' Alex told her with firm assurance.

'How would you know?' Lucy flashed, irritated by his matter-of-fact tone. 'Anybody would think you were an expert on that sort of thing!'

'Maybe I am.' His dark gaze was impassive. 'You don't remember anything at all about last night, do you?' he asked suddenly.

She frowned, staring at the handsome face for a moment before answering. She cradled the warm mug in her hands. 'What do you mean?'

Alex placed his newspaper down on the scrubbed wooden table and stood up. His broad frame seemed to fill the confines of the kitchen. 'Exactly what I say,' he replied, his voice deceptively mild but his dark eyes intent on her face. 'Do you remember anything particular about last night?'

'No.' She watched as he carried his mug across the kitchen, opened the dishwasher, which was beside the deep china sink, and placed his cup inside. 'What sort of thing?' she murmured.

Alex lifted his shoulders in a casual shrug. 'Anything. You tell me.'

'There were some drawers pulled open, and that spare room at the end of the hall looked pretty messy. What happened?' Lucy frowned. 'Did we have burglars or something?'

'No. Nothing like that.' Alex straightened up and looked at her in silence for a couple of seconds. 'You were sleepwalking.'

'I was *what*?' Lucy shook her head quickly. 'No, surely not!' She didn't know why she was bothering to deny it, for she could see, almost *feel* that Alex was telling the truth.

A memory stirred. It had happened before, long ago when she'd been a child; she could remember her mother telling her about it next morning as Alex was doing now, except her mother had laughed about it in her slightly frivolous way, and Alex was staring at her, not looking grim, exactly, but not finding it funny either.

'The thought upsets you?' Dark brows were drawn together. 'Why, exactly?'

'Well...it's kind of...of weird, isn't it?' she muttered. 'At my age anyway.'

'Not particularly. It's just a variant on the dream process,' Alex replied. 'It can happen when a person is particularly wound up about something.'

Lucy released a steadying breath. 'Well, that's me, then, isn't it? I'm as tight as a coiled spring! A total screwball! What was I doing?' she asked, not really wanting to hear the reply but feeling she had to know all the same. 'Something totally ridiculous?'

'Not at all. You were looking for something. Banging drawers and cupboards, searching quite hard. I woke up, heard the noise and wondered what on earth was going on.'

'I made all that mess?' A thought occurred. She looked at him worriedly. 'Did I say anything?'

'You spoke a little, yes,' Alex replied slowly.

A rush of anxiety flooded through her. 'What?' Lucy's voice was sharp with unease. 'What did I say?'

'Just some talk about a shawl. You thought I'd hidden it. Or, rather, not me,' Alex added evenly, 'but the person you thought I was.'

'I've got marks on my legs,' Lucy murmured, glancing down, using the inspection of her shins to hide her embarrassment.

It had been the old dream. The baby was crying because it was cold and she couldn't find the shawl. 'I wondered where the bruises came from.'

'You probably banged them when you were searching. You were quite intense. Let me see.' Alex crouched down in front of her and ran a gentle hand along the line of her shin. 'They look sore. I'll find you some cream later.'

'They're OK.' She moved away from his hands. There was an awkward pause as Alex raised himself. Lucy threw him a hasty glance and added, 'Oh, well, I can't remember any of it!' She tried to keep her voice light, her tone upbeat. 'Sorry if I woke you.'

'Don't be sorry. It was no trouble.'

She met the dark, watchful gaze, trying to gauge something—anything—from his expression. She was scanning her memory frantically, knowing deep down that the exercise was futile. 'So, are you going to give me any details?' she asked. 'I got out of bed and then what?'

'I told you, you were looking for something.'

Heat flooded her face as she thought of something. 'I was in my... nightdress?' she asked cautiously.

'Yes.' There was a slight pause and Lucy knew that he was thinking back, picturing what he had seen—the nightshirt she had brought with her was cool and flimsy; he would have seen more than enough. 'I took you back to your bed, you closed your eyes and went back to sleep.'

'I was asleep already,' she pointed out swiftly.

'You know what I mean,' Alex replied mildly.

'That was it?'

'Isn't that enough?' He turned from her and glanced out of the window. There was more. She knew there was more. 'What have you got planned for today?' Alex continued. 'The weather looks good.'

'You're not telling me everything, are you?'

He turned and looked at her and Lucy knew from his expression that she had guessed right. 'Tell me!' she demanded forcefully. 'Every detail. I have a right to know.'

'And if you don't like what you hear?' Her stomach fluttered in nervous apprehension as Alex walked slowly towards her. He looked down into her upturned face, his dark, intense eyes engaging with uncertain emerald-green. 'What then?'

CHAPTER THREE

'WHAT happened?' Lucy's voice was barely a whisper. She could hardly bear the suspense of not knowing. 'Alex! Please!' She narrowed her eyes in anguish. 'Tell me!'

'Lucy...I think it would be a good idea to talk about your marriage.'

'No!' She frowned, staring at him in horror for a moment, completely thrown by this sudden change of tack. 'No!' Her emerald eyes narrowed warningly and she shook her head vehemently. 'It's a private thing. It's not something I want to discuss with anyone, least of all you!'

'Don't be so defensive. Talking about it will do you good and I'd like to help.'

'You?' Lucy knew that her gaze was full of scorn. Her voice sounded hard, almost bitter, but she couldn't help it. 'I don't need your help,' she asserted forcefully. 'My marriage is none of your concern. Anyway, it's over now. Paul's dead. So what's the point in dragging the memories back to the surface again?'

'You're trying to tell me the memories are buried?' She heard the scathing note in Alex's voice. 'I don't think they are. In fact I think they're positively haunting you. Last night when you were sleepwalking I mentioned Paul's name.'

'What?' Her head shot round, glossy auburn curls shining and bouncing attractively in the sunlight, vivid emerald eyes expressing fear and near-panic as they met the dark, steady gaze.

'You look frantic,' Alex replied evenly. 'I wonder why?'

'What...what did I do?' she blurted out tremulously.

'Your response was surprising, to say the least.' There was a slight pause. His eyes didn't leave her face. 'You acted as if you hated him.'

It was a shock to hear the truth spoken aloud. Nausea settled itself in the pit of Lucy's stomach. Alex was watching her intently and she knew that this was a test of the stiffest kind. 'That . . . that doesn't mean anything,' she mumbled. 'I was asleep! I was having some sort of dream.' She steeled herself and forced a modicum of control back into her voice, turning away so that she didn't have to look into the eyes that seemed to see inside her very soul. 'Paul was my husband,' she added determinedly.

'So?' Strong hands gripped her shoulders and she found herself facing Alex again. 'What's that got to do with anything? The fact is you flinched from me,' he added with cruel precision, 'when you thought I was Paul.'

'No.' The denial hung weakly in the air between them. Lucy dropped her head so that he couldn't see the look of dismay in her eyes. Trust this man, she thought angrily, to discover something that she'd managed to conceal so effectively from everyone else.

'Charles told me you were devastated when Paul was killed,' Alex continued. 'He's under the impression that you loved him madly—'

'I *was* devastated!' she delivered heatedly. 'Of course I was! What sort of a woman do you think I am?'

A dark brow was raised in speculation. 'I don't know—a confused one, perhaps?'

Lucy shook her head, hating Alex Darcy, hating his perception more with each passing second. 'I don't want to talk about it!' she gritted. 'My marriage is—was,' she corrected herself swiftly, 'my own affair. I don't appreciate your interference!'

There was a silence. The only sound that Lucy could hear was the thudding of her heart. She felt sure that if Alex Darcy pushed her any more she would crack.

'There's one more thing about last night that I should tell you.'

'More?' His words halted her thoughts. She was conscious of the sudden lurch in her stomach. 'What happened? What did I do?' She saw a flicker of something in Alex's eyes, an expression that sent a shiver of apprehension through every part of her body. Was he prolonging this agony deliberately?

'You wanted to be kissed.'

'Oh!' Lucy gulped. Her heart went into overdrive. She forced herself to be brave and meet Alex's dark gaze. 'I did?'

'Yes.'

'How embarrassing! Not the sort of thing I do when I'm awake, I can assure you!' She was gabbling like a schoolgirl. She cursed silently and managed an awkward little smile. 'I can't imagine what came over me.' She worked hard at producing a voice which sounded reasonably casual. 'So...what happened? You told yourself I was a crazy, mixed-up kid and took me back to my bed—right?'

'Not quite.' Lucy's heart missed a beat. 'I should have taken you by the hand and led you back to your bed. I *did* do that,' Alex added evenly, 'but not immediately.' He paused and the intensity of his gaze half hinted at what was coming next. 'I told you who I was,' he replied slowly, 'and then...I kissed you.'

She was shocked. The heart that had been pounding fit to burst a moment ago almost stopped completely. Alex Darcy had kissed her and she hadn't even been aware of it...?

'Nothing to say?' There was a thread of amusement in his voice. 'I expected outrage at the very least.'

Lucy looked into the darkly handsome face and wondered if he knew how stupid she felt. 'I don't know what *to* say,' she whispered.

Kiss me again. That was what she wanted to say. Kiss me...

'It's been on my mind,' Alex informed her laconically. 'I have to say I've been feeling bad about it ever since it happened.'

'I see.' He hadn't enjoyed it, then. Lucy tilted her head and worked hard at maintaining some sort of pride. 'Don't worry, I won't hold it against you. I can guess how it was,' she replied stiffly. 'For some mad reason I asked to be kissed and you performed the duty unwillingly, just to keep a deranged sleepwalker on an even keel!' She inhaled a ragged breath and hung her head. 'How embarrassing for you...for me,' she added miserably.

'No!' Alex tilted her chin again so that she had no choice but to look into his face again. 'No,' he repeated slowly, 'it wasn't like that at all.'

'What was it like, then?' Lucy flashed angrily, feeling the heat of humiliation. 'You think I don't know what a pathetic wreck I am—?'

'Like this...' He tugged her close and his mouth was on hers before she even knew what was happening, his lips moving in a slow, sensual rhythm. He tasted wonderful—strong and sure and masculine. Lucy found her own mouth parting in a mixture of astonishment and exhilaration, her eyes closing as delicious sensations assailed the most intimate part of her body.

Alex tugged her close and the touching increased— her hair...her face...her neck... He held her as if it mattered, as if he wanted to feel her, as if he needed her, as if he could never let her go. And all the while his searching mouth was playing havoc with her senses, controlling her mind, so that she couldn't think of anything except the moment and this man...

The jarring sound of the telephone shocked them into stillness and the moment of madness ceased; the promise of endless pleasure came to a sudden and grinding halt. In the too bright, too sunny kitchen the insistent ring seemed to hold some kind of warning. And reality— lonely reality—beckoned as Alex dragged his mouth from hers and thrust her from him as if the feel of her was like poison in his arms.

'Damn!' She watched him bleakly, saw his look of disgust, felt the pain of his curse and the lack of his touch. 'That shouldn't have happened!'

'No.' Was she agreeing with him or denying the assumption that what they had just experienced was wrong? Lucy didn't know, hardly cared. She felt humiliated and bemused, but, worst of all, desperately, desperately disappointed.

Alex walked to the phone and picked up the receiver, his eyes still on her face. 'Yes?' He listened to the voice on the other end, dark eyes devouring her without respite. After a moment he held his hand over the receiver and said, 'It's Charles. Would you like to speak to him?'

Lucy shook her head. 'No.' She couldn't pretend now. She didn't have the energy to put on a cheerful voice and make Charles believe that everything was all right. How could it be, with Alex looking at her as if she were some kind of living curse?

'Are you sure?' Alex frowned. He spoke into the phone. 'Just a minute, Charles; I'll see if I can find her.' A large hand was placed over the receiver again. Dark eyes speared Lucy's face. 'He'd like to know how you are.'

'You tell him, then!'

'He'd prefer to hear it from you.'

'Alex...' Her voice trembled precariously, but she persisted, spelling the words out slowly and precisely. 'I cannot talk to Charles now!'

'OK.' Alex's mouth firmed into a hard line. He inhaled deeply and, turning his back, proceeded to speak into the phone. 'Sorry, Charles, Lucy's just stepped into the shower...'

She listened for a moment. It was amazing how cool Alex sounded, she thought. He had blasted all practical thought from her mind and yet here he was, talking to Charles as if nothing had happened.

She walked to the kitchen door, opened it and then banged it shut behind her with considerable force. Even outside she could still hear him talking. She paced outside on the terrace, plucking an orange distractedly from an overhanging branch, raising the fruit to her nose to smell the clear, sharp, citrus aroma. Why did everything always have to be complicated? Was she jinxed—was that what it was? Would she continue for the rest of her life to fall always for the wrong kind of men? The breath caught in her throat. Was that what she'd done—fallen for him?

She sat down heavily on a wooden seat situated beneath the window of the kitchen and closed her eyes, trying hard to relax.

She could hear Alex's voice through the open window—deep and mellow. She pictured his face, remembered the taste of his mouth on hers...

'Charles, I'm an author; that's my profession now—' He sounded tense, a little edgy. Maybe, Lucy thought, their kiss had affected him just as much as it had her. 'Well, don't expect too much... Yes... Yes, I know, but you're shouldering me with too much responsibility.' There was a pause.

She listened properly for the first time and wondered why the word 'responsibility' should feature in Alex's conversation with Charles. Responsibility—was that what she was? And 'expect'. Why should Charles expect anything?

Lucy wondered what her stepbrother was saying. Listening in on other people's phone calls wasn't the sort of thing she usually did, but somehow the one-sided conversation was difficult to ignore...

'God knows, I'm not a saint, Charles; you know that better than anyone...' Lucy moved restlessly on the seat. She knew that she should move away, but somehow the words insisted on being heard. 'Look, she's got one hell of a lot of problems to work through...' A pause. Lucy gripped the edge of the wooden seat and told herself that Alex's last sentence was a punishment for eavesdropping. 'Damn you, Charles! It was a long time ago; I've left that part of my life behind. I told you that in the very beginning. You cannot expect me to—' She heard Alex release a taut breath. 'OK. As long as we've got that much clear... Yes... Speak to you soon.'

Lucy kept her position. When Alex came out onto the terrace a few moments later, presumably to give her a watered-down version of the telephone call, she spoke in crisp, hard tones. 'You were discussing me with Charles.'

She had expected him to appear uncomfortable, but when he turned towards her there was only the slightest hint of surprise in his expression. 'He asked how you were.'

'Oh, come on!' she replied tightly. 'There was more to it than just a casual enquiry. You were discussing me! I heard you!'

'And if we were?' His eyes narrowed a little. 'That upsets you?'

'Of course it does!' Lucy, unable to sit still a moment longer, got up and paced angrily up and down the terrace again. 'Of course!'

'Why?'

Lucy gulped a breath, staring with fixed anguish into Alex's infuriatingly relaxed face. '"Why?" "Why?" It just does, OK? You've been probing and prying into my private affairs ever since I arrived here and I'm sick of it!'

'Oh, give me a break!' Alex exhaled and shook his head in exasperation. 'That's not true and you know it!'

'Isn't it?'

'I'm not about to enter into an argument over this!' Alex threw her an impatient look. 'Eavesdropping is not a clever thing to do!'

'So what did my dear stepbrother have to say?' Lucy flashed. She bit her lip. The image of them a moment ago, together in each other's arms, wouldn't go away. She could still taste his kiss, remember the scent of his skin, the roughness of his arms as he had held her close...

'Not a great deal.' Alex lifted his shoulders in a belated shrug and then turned and looked out across the valley, which stretched invitingly below.

'Did you tell him you'd taken advantage of his kid sister?'

'I'd *what*?' Alex spun back round, staring at Lucy as if she were mad.

That had had the desired effect, she thought. 'You heard!' she croaked. She tilted her chin in an attempt at defiance. 'You took advantage of me—last night, a few moments ago! It's obvious Charles trusts you, but he hasn't a clue, has he? Maybe I should tell him just what sort of a friend you really are!'

She knew that she was going too far, but something inside drove her on—some madness. She had been so meek and mild with Paul; what was making her act this way now? Maybe it was some sort of release—a safety valve that just needed to blow its top.

Alex crossed the terrace towards her. He looked formidable, anger darkening his eyes, hardening his mouth. If looks could kill...she thought anxiously.

'Do you *want* me to seduce you? Is that what this is all about?'

He took her breath away with his audacity. Lucy tried to think of a scathing retort but she was caught off balance by the cold, calm voice that had spoken aloud the very thought that she had been avoiding ever since she had arrived in northern Majorca.

'No!' Her voice was a whispered breath.

'I don't believe you.' His gaze was direct. A hand reached out. Strong, tantalising fingers stroked the bare skin of her arm. Tormenting her. Teaching her a lesson with the lightest of touches.

'Why should I care what you believe?' Lucy replied with unconvincing vigour. 'You're...you're an arrogant man and I wish I'd never set eyes on you. Now, if you'll excuse me,' she added shakily, conscious that what little control she had left wasn't going to last much longer. She moved to go past him, but the fingers that had been light and teasing on her arm suddenly gripped and held her firm.

'Lucy...'

She saw the flicker of sympathy in the dark gaze and felt humiliation rise. 'Don't say anything!'

He ignored her advice. 'Kissing you a moment ago felt like the right thing to do. It wasn't planned; it wasn't premeditated—'

'You pulled away as if the sight and the touch of me repelled you!' she muttered unsteadily, conscious of a swift ache deep within—regret and desire all rolled into one.

'I pulled away for a totally different reason and you know it!' Alex gritted. 'Why are you making this so difficult?'

'I...I...' She hardly knew what to think, what to feel any more.

'I have a responsibility,' he asserted. 'Charles expects me to take care of you. He expects me to do what's right.'

'And what is right?' Lucy queried unsteadily, lifting her face to look into his eyes. 'Ignoring me? Arguing with me? Turning me inside out and upside down? Am I supposed to feel *good* because you rejected me so effectively?'

'It matters that I did?' Alex asked quietly.

'Rejection always hurts!' she retorted swiftly, conscious that she was in danger of giving too much away. 'No matter what direction it comes from!'

'You've had your fair share?'

Lucy returned his challenging look directly. 'Yes.' She hesitated, and when Alex made no reply she went on swiftly, 'My mother left our family when I was six. I lived with a father who barely knew night from day for two years. I got by, wondering what I'd done wrong, trying to imagine why Mummy had suddenly decided she didn't love me or my father any more.' She paused, but only briefly—if she stopped to think about what she was saying ... 'The two of us were going quietly insane.'

'Then your father married Charles's mother,' Alex said quietly.

'That's right.' She gulped a breath and added awkwardly, 'It's not all doom and gloom. She saved us, and she was kind to me. She wasn't my mother, of course, but better than nothing. Charles was a lot older, but he took the time to make friends with his new stepsister.' She shrugged. 'I don't know why I'm telling you this...'

'And then your father and stepmother were killed in a road accident,' Alex continued for her grimly. 'And you lost everyone again.'

'Except Charles.' Lucy attempted a smile that didn't quite come off. 'It happens,' she murmured.

'Did you marry Paul soon after that?'

She threw him a cautious look. This was the last thing that she had imagined they would be discussing. But somehow it felt right. 'A few weeks, yes.'

'You felt alone. You needed someone. What about your real mother?' Alex pressed. 'Where is she?'

Lucy felt the twist of pain. Would she ever get over it? she wondered. 'She emigrated to Australia. I haven't heard from her in ... oh, in ten years.'

'Have you tried to make contact?'

'Once. Just after the road accident.' Lucy's voice was hard and brittle. 'She's got another life; she didn't want to know. It's over. I don't want to talk about it!' She struggled to free herself from Alex's hold but he held her without effort. 'Would you let go of my arm, please?' she enquired harshly.

'Tell me about Paul.'

'No!' She shook her head violently. 'There's nothing to tell! He's dead. He's buried. I don't want to think about him any more!'

'Do you miss him?'

She looked away, shaking her head a little at the directness of the question. What should she say? No? Yes? I'm not sure? Misery locked in her throat. If she told Alex the truth, then everyone would know what a sham her marriage had been. And he would probe and pry and before she knew where she was she would be telling Alex everything. About the verbal torture and the drinking and the gambling and the baby... and then he would report back to Charles and the whole world would know what a mess she had made of her life.

'That's none of your business!' she gritted.

'Why can't you admit you had an unhappy marriage?' Alex asked quietly. 'Was it that bad?'

'Stop it!' Lucy flared. 'Leave my marriage out of this! It's got nothing to do with you!'

'I want to help.'

'No, you don't!' she cried. 'You just want to interfere. You're curious, that's all it is. Charles asked you to find out the grisly details, so that you can report back to him.'

Alex's expression held derision. 'Now you're acting paranoid!' he replied. 'For goodness' sake—!'

She raised her hand and hit him before he finished speaking. The slap rang out in the still of the morning— a sharp, dramatic sound that made Lucy gasp aloud as if she herself had been struck.

She stared in horror. 'I'm sorry... I...I don't know...' Her voice trailed away. She could see the red marks where her fingers had made contact high on his strong cheekbone. She shook her head, hardly able to comprehend her own actions. She had *hit* him?

'All this anger should have been expressed before.' Alex looked savage. The dark eyes were sharp and watchful in his taut, angular face. 'Paul's the one you're really mad at; why take it out on me?'

'Because you're here and he's not!' Lucy choked. 'That's why!'

'I'll not be your whipping boy,' Alex growled. 'You'd better remember that. Push me too far and you'll discover I can instantly forget the meaning of words such as patience and responsibility!'

And, with that dire warning ringing in her ears, he released her from his hold, turned on his heel and left the terrace. Leaving Lucy to contemplate the possible fate that awaited her if she continued to cross swords with Alex Darcy.

CHAPTER FOUR

ALEX had told Lucy that he led a secluded life and she believed him. For two days she believed him, whilst they avoided one another and she spent her time lying around in the sun feeling restless and desperately unhappy.

On the third day, Alex put in an unexpected appearance and destroyed the myth he had created.

Lucy had just finished eating breakfast alone on the terrace as usual. The sun was warm and she was trying her hardest to relax.

'Found something you like?'

Lucy sneaked a look. Alex stood at the end of the sun-lounger, looming large, arms folded across his broad chest. He was wearing a faded denim shirt, undone at the neck, rolled up at the sleeves, and a pair of cut-off jeans. She caught sight of acres of muscled, bronzed flesh and quickly lowered her eyes to her book again.

Make him wait! she told herself. Hadn't he treated her as if she were barely visible over the last couple of days? Going into his study at the crack of dawn, not emerging again until dusk. A civil nod here, a casual reply there...

'Must be a riveting book,' Alex drawled. 'What chapter are you on?'

Lucy succeeded in playing it cool for all of ten seconds. She raised her head slowly, not knowing how to combat the feeling of excitement that his presence produced.

'It is.' She flicked through a couple of pages. Alex's eyes were dark and formidable, and although his enquiry had sounded casual enough a chill ran through her veins, despite the warmth of the morning, as she caught the expression in his eyes. 'And I'm on chapter three.' Lucy threw him a wintry smile. She hadn't read a word.

She'd just grabbed the first volume off the shelf in the sitting room on her way outside. There was a tense pause. 'Was there something you particularly wanted?' she asked with saccharine sweetness. 'Or are you just admiring the view?'

He didn't like her tone; she could see that. Lucy didn't like it either, but it seemed the best, the *only* one to take in the circumstances. She closed the book, placing it on her lap, gripping the cover tightly, watching as Alex turned and looked down at the valley. She still hadn't got over his kiss. She still hadn't got over the fact that it had felt wonderful to be in his arms. She still couldn't believe that she had been fool enough to hit him...

'I'm having a few people over this evening.' He turned slowly and looked down at her. 'Of course you needn't feel obliged to attend; you may want to stay in your room whilst they're here.'

It took a couple of seconds for the information to sink in, for the implications of what Alex had said to register fully. 'Are you *telling* me to stay in my room?' Lucy enquired, her brows drawing together in a frown. 'Is that what you're saying?'

'No.' Jet-black eyes held her face. She could somehow sense the effort that Alex needed to keep his voice on an even keel, despite the fact that his face gave little enough away. 'I'm just giving you notice of their arrival, that's all. After the tranquillity you've experienced here, it may come as something of a shock to have an influx of people—'

'*Tranquillity?*' Her voice held scorn.

'Relative tranquillity,' he replied crisply. 'You've had peace for the past two days whilst I've been working in my study, haven't you?'

Did he really believe that? Lucy wondered, thinking of the hours she had spent going over and over their most recent of confrontations.

'The guests will be arriving around eight.' He eyed her impassively. 'As I've said, you shouldn't feel obliged to attend.'

'I won't.' Lucy thought she saw a flicker of relief cross Alex's face, but she wasn't sure. Didn't he want her around, then—mingling with his friends, chatting to them? Why? Was he ashamed of her? The thought was a depressing one. And the more she dwelt upon it, the more certain she became that that was the correct reason for this weakly veiled attempt to keep her away. He didn't care that she knew it either, and that hurt too.

'You think I'm trying to insult you?' He shook his head slightly and managed, with that smallest of gestures, to convey a provocative amount of scorn and derision. 'They're good people,' he continued brusquely. 'But they're lively. The party was arranged before you came to stay.' Cool eyes scanned her face. 'I'm beginning to think I should have cancelled.'

'Oh, don't ruin your social life on my account!' Lucy replied sharply. 'I get the picture. You're worried that I'll cramp your style, that I'll be an embarrassment!'

'Don't be ridiculous!' Alex stared at her as if she were stupid. 'Do you have to be so obtuse? I'll cancel,' he added briskly.

'What, and let all your friends down?' Lucy glared up at him. 'Oh, no! I'd really feel like I'm an inconvenience then, wouldn't I? Bad enough that I've been foisted onto you at such short notice, without my presence hindering your social life as well!'

'You really are determined to be difficult, aren't you?' he delivered conversationally.

'How am I being difficult?' she queried, widening her emerald eyes innocently. 'I thought I just said—'

'It's clear that whatever I say is going to be misinterpreted.' Alex raised two hands in irritation as Lucy made as if to say more. 'I don't want to get into another argument. Come if you wish. Otherwise, I'll make it clear

to everyone at the beginning that the party will be ending
at a respectable hour.'

'I can stay up past ten o'clock, you know!' she replied
testily. 'I haven't had a curfew placed on me.'

'Will you be attending or not?' Alex's eyes grazed her
face. Then his gaze lowered and his eyes roamed her
body, and Lucy was suddenly aware of just how tightly
her cotton shorts fitted and how brief her cropped sun-
top was, scarcely covering the curve of her breasts. She
shifted self-consciously on the sun-lounger.

Alex's eyes gleamed as if he recognised her discomfort. He reached forward and Lucy's heart jolted
violently. Touching was on her mind. Forty-eight hours
with only the memory of how it had felt to be held by
him—it felt like a lifetime.

Tenacious fingers picked up the book from Lucy's lap.
Disappointment, mingled with annoyance, speared
through her body as Alex deliberately avoided physical
contact. The volume looked small and insignificant in
his large hands. She watched, frowning a little as he
opened a page. 'A woman of many talents, I see!' Dark
eyes gleamed knowingly as he tossed the book back towards her, and she caught it without a second thought.
'I had no idea you were good at reading Spanish!'

Lucy glanced down at the volume in her hand and
cursed as a series of incomprehensible words stared back
at her.

The guests started arriving a little after eight, just as Alex
had said they would. Car after car became visible from
her bedroom window, sweeping up the dusty track and
invading the tranquil peace of the valley.

There were around forty people. Lucy watched nervously as a quite bizarre mix of people entered Alex's
domain at intervals—young, bright girls, older, casually
dressed men and women, sophisticated, trendy types and
older, comfortable-looking locals. All, it seemed to Lucy,

possessed the sort of casual, relaxed attitude which she could only dream about.

She watched the party's progress from the safety of her bedroom, careful not to be seen, hiding herself behind the fall of curtains. She smoothed her dress with trembling fingers and tried to gather her resolve as lively music and laughing voices floated up from the terrace below. It would be a test of her character if she ever made it out of this room, she realised. Mixing with these loud, confident people would not be easy, especially with Alex having already sapped any enthusiasm she might have had for the occasion.

She rose and walked towards the full-length mirror in the bedroom. Her appearance didn't do a great deal to bolster her confidence. She looked young—the word 'sweet' sprang to mind, but Lucy thrust it away quickly, almost scornfully. How could she possibly be sweet with her chequered history? Haunted. Now, that was certainly true. Lucy raised a hand and smoothed it across her furrowed brow. Tension was making her head ache.

Her outfit wasn't up to much. The fact that it was silk and still possessed the fluid movement of that fabric, skimming Lucy's slim figure gracefully, was the only thing going for it, she decided. It was short—too short, maybe, barely covering the middle of her thighs—and the colour had faded dreadfully over the years. Once upon a time it had been the most gorgeous mauve—the colour of asters in September; now the fabric resembled the purplish tinge visible beneath her eyes, which was testament to countless sleepless nights.

Still, it would have to do, as would her cream canvas espadrilles. Lucy released a tense breath and cautiously opened the door of her bedroom. Laughter floated up the stairway. She heard the chink of glasses and the sound of many conversations all taking place at once. She hovered, searching for her courage, willing herself to make the first move, to step out of the sanctuary of her room.

Alex was down there somewhere. She closed her eyes and pictured herself in fantasy land—talking to him, laughing, smiling, him smiling in return. The need to lay eyes on him was overwhelming suddenly, as strong, stronger than the idea of proving a point about whether she attended his party or not. She wanted things to be right between them. She hated the fact that somehow her usual placid nature twisted itself into something bitter and totally alien whenever he got within striking range.

Lucy inhaled deeply. Gripping the rope rail tightly, she began to descend the stairs, aware, with each step, that she had never felt so alone in all her life.

The kitchen was heaving; food and drink was clearly uppermost in the great majority of minds. Maria, Alex's housekeeper from the village, had done him proud; there were huge bowls full of delicious-looking food covering every available surface, along with a hundred and one bottles of all shapes and colours.

Making progress through the room was difficult. She squeezed and ducked through the crowd. The doorway to the terrace was like light at the end of a tunnel, and she was just congratulating herself on reaching her destination when the light dimmed and she looked up to find Alex's broad frame blocking her way.

'I thought you weren't going to come down.' There was a shot of steel in his voice. 'I thought you had decided you wanted nothing to do with all this.'

Lucy ran her tongue nervously over her lips. 'I don't remember saying that,' she replied, raising her voice above the high-spirited conversations that were taking place all around them.

Her gaze fell from his face, was drawn irresistibly to his body. She had a sensation of floating dizziness, although no alcohol had passed her lips. He looked incredible. Intoxicating. Sharp. Rugged. Undeniably handsome. He was dressed in well-cut black trousers which accentuated the slimness of his hips and the solid power of his thighs and a crisp, white shirt, left casually unbuttoned at his neck, revealing a tanned throat, the hint of his broad chest with its smattering of dark, curly hair...

Alex didn't look happy, and that somehow made him all the more irresistible.

He had a tumbler in one hand. Lucy's gaze rested briefly on the amber liquid swirling in the bottom of the glass. Then it was being raised to the formidable mouth and consumed as if Alex were in a desert and dying of thirst.

'Don't look so aghast,' he drawled, placing the empty glass on a stone ledge beside the door. 'That was my first drink of the evening.'

Something was wrong. Lucy frowned and wondered what it was.

'I was just about to come up and see you,' Alex informed her coolly. 'I thought you were doing the sensible thing and staying in your room.'

She inhaled a small, steadying breath. 'Me? Sensible?' She managed a smile. 'Alex—'

He shook his head. 'It's OK. Forget it. I'm as much to blame for the way things have been between us.'

'But I...I hit you.' Lucy lowered her voice, frowning as she said the words. 'I never meant to—'

'I said forget it.' Alex's gaze was warm and intense. 'As far as I'm concerned, it never happened. You're looking good.' His eyes moved downwards from her face to cover her body with a slow appraisal—a dark, dangerous gaze that did nothing for Lucy's powers of self-control. 'You've made quite an effort,' he remarked. 'I haven't seen that dress before.'

'It's old,' she declared, 'but it's the best I've got.' She saw his gaze linger on the simple round neckline, then move to the hem swirling around the middle of her tanned thighs.

'It's short,' he pointed out.

'What's the matter? Don't you like it?' she asked daringly.

'Would it make a difference if I said no?' He smiled seductively. 'Would you go up and change into something less...?'

'Less what?' She challenged him with her eyes.

'Less provocative.' His voice was taut again. The dark head shook slightly. 'I'm not sure I want you here now.'

Lucy frowned. 'Why not?' Her voice was hard. How could he say that to her? 'Look, I won't embarrass you, if that's what you're worried about! I won't drink too much and say all the wrong things to all the right people!' She turned and glanced briefly around the kitchen, recognising a few interested looks. 'I am capable of adult behaviour, despite what you so clearly think!'

'I know that.' Alex's look revealed impatience. He released a taut breath, dragging lean, strong hands through his dark hair. 'It's not you I'm worried about...'

Lucy watched the gesture and felt the jolt of attraction. 'So what's the matter, then?' she asked.

Dark eyes narrowed. 'Who said anything was the matter?'

She shifted her slender shoulders in a shrug. 'You don't seem particularly relaxed,' she murmured. 'I can't believe it's just because I've chosen to make an appearance.'

'No, you're right.' Alex released a short breath. 'I've just heard they're filming a book of mine in the next valley.' His dark gaze roamed restlessly around the room.

'And that makes you uptight?' Lucy queried.

'Remember the car that nearly shunted us off the road?'

'Yes, of course.' She watched his face carefully. 'What about it?'

'It seemed too much of a coincidence at the time, but now I'm pretty sure it was the person I half suspected it was.' Dark brows drew together in a frown. He looked displeased. No, more than that, Lucy thought; he looked angry—deeply angry.

She waited a moment. When Alex didn't continue, she prompted cautiously, 'And is there some connection—between the filming and the driver of the car?'

'It's a possibility.' His tone was abrupt. 'It's certainly beginning to look that way. The man I have in mind is a director,' he explained briefly, noticing her puzzlement.

'Is he here?' She remembered the people around them and glanced with interest around the room.

'No. I don't think he'd be quite so stupid as to put in an appearance. Although, you never can tell. He's got a pretty thick skin.'

'You don't like him,' Lucy murmured quietly, wondering what on earth this nameless man could have done to evoke such cold, hard hatred.

'No.' Alex looked down at her pale face. 'But there's no need for you to look so anxious.' He smiled. 'It's my problem. I'll deal with it, if and when I have to.' He grabbed her hand suddenly and she saw that he was making an effort to drag himself out of his melancholy. 'Come on.'

His touch was like an electric shock. Lucy felt her heart thud as his strong fingers linked intimately with hers. 'Where to?'

'Outside. It's a wonderful evening.'

Alex led her through the mêlée by the door out into the warm night air. Lights had been strung in haphazard fashion around the terrace. A few other couples were already entwined together in the evening light, dancing to the haunting, melodious tune which emanated from strategically placed speakers.

Dark eyes enslaved her. Alex held both her hands and pulled her towards him. 'Dance with me.'

Her heart pounded like a steam train. 'Is that a request or an order?' she queried shakily.

'What do you think?' His mouth flicked into a curve and he pulled her with absolute authority into his arms.

'You're supposed to ask,' she croaked, holding herself rigid, looking up into his handsome face. 'Maybe I don't want to dance.'

'No?' His expression revealed deliberate surprise. 'Isn't this what parties are all about?' he murmured. 'Isn't this why you're down here? Besides,' he added smoothly, 'it was too crowded in the kitchen. And I want to keep an eye on you.' He moved her closer to him and this time she offered no resistance. His hand was firm at the small of her back. She could feel the strength of his fingers through the flimsy fabric of her dress. 'Relax!' he murmured against the sweep of her hair. 'I'm not the swine you think I am.'

Excitement scorched along Lucy's veins. She had to keep cool, she thought. She mustn't respond to the desire which moved restlessly within. Alex was touching her and it felt like nothing else on earth, but she had to keep her self-control. She could barely breathe. She melted against him, succumbing to the sound of his voice. She tried desperately hard to concentrate on the music, the lights, the now shadowy view from the terrace, but it all floated over her head. By turning slightly she could see the other figures moving silently around them in the warm evening light, but they were in another world. The only dimension that mattered at this moment was the one she shared with Alex. As they swayed together, touched each other she was bound to him within the circle of his arms; she could feel the warmth of his body against hers, the intimate nature of each curve, each limb.

It was torture dancing with him like this, wanting him so much, despising herself for wanting him...

The music came to an end. There was no longer an excuse for being so close. Lucy tried to pull away. She didn't want the false intimacy of this embrace, she told herself. It was nothing to Alex, but it meant too much to her. Far too much.

He resisted her movement, preventing her departure with casual strength, his hand sliding from her back to her waist. She felt the broad expanse of his chest as he held her close. 'Stay with me.'

Lucy's stomach flipped. *'What?'* she whispered, hardly daring to believe what she'd heard.

'I don't want you straying this evening. I don't want any big, bad strangers giving you grief.' Alex lowered his head before Lucy could make any kind of reply and gently brushed her lips with his own. 'Trust me,' he murmured. 'I just want to look after you.'

Tears misted her eyes. She thanked heaven it was evening and practically dark. She felt a sudden, over-whelming urge to throw her arms around Alex's neck and hug him tight, to press her body against his, to feel his warmth and his power, to never let him go. 'I . . . I can look after myself, you know,' she croaked.

'Humour me, will you?' Alex's voice was husky and compelling. 'You look far too vulnerable tonight. I think I'll tell everyone to go home. I don't want them here.'

'You can't do that. They've only just arrived.'

'Oh, I can.' Dark eyes gleamed down at her. 'Believe me, it would be the easiest thing in the world.'

'No!' Lucy swallowed the lump in her throat. She had thought she could be strong, but she hadn't counted on Alex talking to her like this. He sounded so wonderfully sincere, as if he meant every word, every wonderful look. But he couldn't, could he? What was it? Just party talk? The easy, seductive patter of a man who liked to control?

She needed space, time to take all this in, to compose herself. Upstairs in her bedroom this had been her fantasy, and now that it was happening she was lost. When did fantasy and reality ever coincide?

'Do you think I could have a drink?' she ventured shakily. 'I feel terribly thirsty.'

He was looking down at her with an odd expression. A look she wasn't capable of interpreting shadowed his face. Alex released a taut breath. 'OK. If that's what you want.'

Lucy nodded firmly. 'It is.'

'What would you like?'

'I...I don't mind,' she whispered, wondering about the hint of annoyance in his voice. 'Anything.'

'Come and sit over here, then.' He led her by the hand to the edge of the terrace. 'I'll be back in a moment. Don't move!' he added. 'I'll introduce you to a few people in a minute.'

Lucy sat on the rough stone wall and watched Alex thread his way through the guests who were spilling out from the house. He was detained once or twice and she found herself soaking up every gesture, every movement as he paused to talk. She saw him look back towards her and felt a warm glow as his gaze lingered. Then he disappeared into the house, and Lucy finally found the strength to breathe properly.

The terrace became quiet. The other couples drifted off towards the house, presumably in search of food or drink. Two made their way down the steps into the orchard beyond, their arms entwined around one another, in search of far more sensual pleasures.

She leant back against the wall and watched the moving through the evening light, kissing and moving, the girl resting her head on her companion's shoulder as they walked.

Lucy closed her eyes. Imagination could be a wonderful thing. Soon she and Alex were following in their footsteps, enjoying the same glorious intimacies together—laughing, talking, kissing, making love...

'Well, hello! Not asleep, surely? I thought Alex's parties were far better than that!'

The voice, lazy and distinct with a clear American drawl, was close. Lucy's eyes flicked open and she turned in startled embarrassment. She had been so intent on praying that fantasy and reality would collide once again that she hadn't been aware of anyone approaching.

'Sorry, did I startle you?' Gleaming brown eyes met her gaze. Lucy blinked. A sharp, multicoloured shirt almost blinded her. Lime-green and purple—a striking choice.

'No...no, it's all right.' She looked upwards into a face that was long and lean and full of charm and humour.

The smiling, over-indulgent mouth widened. Limp blonde hair fell over one eye and was casually flicked back with a negligent hand. 'You were miles away. Sweet dreams, were they?' Calculating brown eyes flicked up and down, taking in the faded dress, the down-at-heel espadrilles, the tumble of glowing auburn hair that fell almost to Lucy's waist. 'I'm Jeff.' A slim, tanned hand was held out towards her. 'You are...?'

Lucy took a breath and held out her own hand. 'Lucy,' she murmured. 'Lucy Harper.'

'Well, pleased to meet you, Lucy Harper!' An unmistakably expensive Rolex watch glittered at his wrist. He turned and glanced at the illuminated house. 'How's the party going?'

'Fine, I think.' She followed his glance. 'Everyone seems to be enjoying themselves.'

'I hope he hasn't deserted you.' Lucy frowned slightly and Jeff added smoothly, 'I saw you and Alex dancing just now. Very intimate, I must say.' The attractive mouth twisted. 'Known each other long, have you?'

Lucy wasn't sure how to answer that. She found herself blushing faintly. 'Not very, no. Alex has just gone to get me a drink,' she added. 'He'll be back in a moment.'

'So you're not close friends, then?'

'I...I don't think we've ever been friends,' Lucy replied cautiously.

'No?' Brown eyes lingered on her face with interest. 'No? More than that, maybe. He always was a fast mover; I'll say that for Alex.' There was a flash of white teeth and an infectious smile lit up the handsome face. 'Don't mind me; I just like to get my facts straight. Makes for less complication later on. Now let me guess!'

He gave Lucy a deliberate scrutiny. 'You're a model—right?'

Lucy frowned. Her thoughts were still with Alex. She wanted more time to dwell on their dance, on the way he had held her, on that look—that wonderfully powerful look that hinted at ravishment and possession and a hundred and one other totally impossible things. 'Er...no. What on earth makes you say that?' she asked, frowning, hardly aware of the other man's interested gaze.

'Too modest!' Her companion grinned affably. 'A girl with your looks! So what *do* you do?' he continued. 'Butcher? Baker? Candlestick-maker?'

'Oh . . . well, nothing much at present.' Lucy cursed inwardly. She really was acting like a moonstruck idiot! Pull yourself together! she admonished herself silently. 'I'm not in any business at the moment. I'm taking a...a holiday.'

'With Alex.'

Lucy hesitated a moment, then nodded. 'Yes.'

Jeff looked at her consideringly. 'You have the most wonderful hair. I don't think I've seen anyone as beautiful as you in a long while.'

'You haven't?' Lucy didn't try to hide her shock or her amazement. This was a most peculiar conversation. She looked at Jeff, inspecting his face for signs of sincerity. 'I don't think that...' She shook her head, lost for words. 'No one's ever said anything like that to me before,' she added regretfully.

'Not even Alex?' Jeff waited, watching Lucy's expression carefully. When she made no reply he sat beside her on the wall and added conversationally, 'Don't fancy being in a movie, do you? It's not a chat-up line, honestly,' he put in quickly. 'But I saw you sitting here all on your own... You know, you have got a look of...' he shrugged, smiling all the while, putting her at her ease ' . . . of angelic beauty.'

Lucy released a nervous laugh. She couldn't help it. It was incredibly difficult not to respond to the infectious grin. 'You're talking rubbish!' she accused him. 'And that has to be the worst chat-up line I've ever heard!' She smiled and shook her head, a great deal more relaxed suddenly.

'So, you're trying to tell me that with your looks, your figure, your hair and that wonderful voice you've never even considered acting as a possibility?' Jeff persisted in easy tones. 'I can't believe it!'

Lucy hesitated. 'Well...' she began, 'I did attend stage school for a while.'

'Ah!' Brown eyes sparkled in the evening light. 'It's my lucky night! You *can* act.'

'Not really.' Lucy felt uncomfortable suddenly, wishing that she hadn't mentioned it. She glanced towards the house and wondered where Alex was. 'I mean, nothing much came of it. It started out OK, but then it all sort of fell away.'

'Really?' Interested eyes kept up the pressure. 'Why was that?'

Lucy looked blank. She felt out of her depth. She glanced sideways and then hung her head, twisting the fabric of her dress between two fingers. 'Oh, you don't want to know,' she murmured. 'It's not very interesting.'

'Of course it is! There must have been some pretty extenuating circumstances for a girl with your potential not to have succeeded. Believe me, if there's one thing I know about, it's talent,' Jeff replied, contemplating Lucy intently.

'Well...' Lucy began awkwardly, 'I—'

'Interrogating my guest, Jeff?' The voice was crisp, edged with steel.

Lucy's head shot up. Alex was standing before them with a glass in each hand. He gave one to Lucy without a word or a look. She took it and her hands shook, because suddenly there was tension—an atmosphere so thick that it could almost be cut with a knife.

A thought stirred in Lucy's brain. This was the man he hated. 'And gatecrashing too? I didn't think that was your style.'

'Ah, Alex!' The bonhomie was overdone and clearly false. Alex looked as if murder was on his mind. 'Great party! Thought I'd drop by, as I was so close.' The large mouth widened into a grin again. 'Lucy and I have been getting to know one another!' Jeff threw Alex a knowing smile. 'She tells me she's always wanted to be an actress!'

'You said that?' Alex's gaze flicked across and Lucy felt the full force of his displeasure. Hard, cold eyes looked at her as if she were a traitor.

'I didn't say that exactly,' Lucy murmured tensely. She swallowed some wine and tried not to be intimidated. 'I just mentioned that I'd attended stage school.' She forced herself to meet his gaze. 'Jeff was just being sociable.' She pursed her lips together and flashed Alex a defiant glance. 'What's wrong with that?'

'What's wrong...?' Alex shook his head as if he couldn't believe that she could be so stupid. His eyes flicked towards Jeff once again. 'This man wouldn't know "sociable" if it reared up and hit him in the face! You've got a nerve!' he gritted. 'Turning up here—'

'Alex, please!' Lucy frowned. 'Do you have to be *so* unpleasant? This is a party; don't...' She hesitated, hating the hard look in his eyes. He was like a stranger suddenly. 'Don't spoil everything.'

'Lucy, keep out of this!' The words were clipped and icy. 'You don't understand.'

'Now, do I get the impression that my presence has caused friction between you two?' Jeff stood up, holding his hands out in an apologetic gesture. 'I'm sure that was never my intention.'

'No?' Alex's voice was frosted with ice. 'Somehow I find that hard to believe.'

'Come on Alex!' Jeff's smile was pure friendship. 'I'm trying to wave a white flag here! Why do you think I came? After all this time we still can't bury the hatchet?'

'Oh, I'd like to bury the hatchet!' Alex's eyes speared Jeff's face. 'But I don't think now is the time or the place.' He turned and surveyed the surrounding area. Guests were mingling. Laughter filled the air. Just a few feet away, people were dancing to a lively tune. It all seemed, Lucy thought, dreadfully incongruous. 'As you can see, I'm having a party.' Alex turned back towards Jeff again and cold anger filled his face. 'You weren't invited. Lucy—' Alex flicked a cold glance in her direction '—I suggest you go inside. There's food in the kitchen. Get yourself another drink.'

It was a cold, hard dismissal and she hated it. She glanced from Alex to Jeff. The latter's smile, she noted, had slipped, so that it now resembled more of a grimace. Clearly he didn't like Alex's tone any more than she did. Anger stirred in Lucy's veins. He had made her feel uptight and foolish and she wasn't prepared to put up with it.

'Best do as he says.' Jeff threw her a warm smile. 'Alex can be particularly ruthless.' The brown eyes narrowed as he looked across at him. 'It's a trait he picked up at birth; he'll never grow out of it.'

'Nor would I want to! Get into the house, Lucy!' Alex said sharply.

'Don't order me about!' She hated him talking to her like this. She wouldn't have it. She wouldn't! Not after Paul and all his bullying.

Dark eyes scoured her face. He didn't have to speak; it was all there—cold command in every line, every angle...

'Be careful, Lucy!' Jeff warned, watching the interchange. 'With Alex you only get one chance.'

'And ours is just about all used up!' Alex moved towards Jeff. His large hand shot out and gripped the collar of Jeff's shirt. 'Get out! Before I throw you out!'

'OK! OK! I'm going!' Jeff forced a grin as the other party-goers turned and stared. 'No need to resort to violence!'

Lucy closed her eyes. Violence. She felt sick. She stood up and placed her glass carefully on the top of the wall. Alex looked at her, but she avoided his gaze. 'I'll show you out, Jeff,' she murmured shakily. 'It's on my way.' She forced as much strength into her voice as she could muster. 'It seems Alex wants us both to leave his party.'

'Lucy!'

Alex's voice was insistent, but somehow she resisted. She placed one foot in front of another and crossed the terrace with her head bowed.

'Where are you going?' Alex caught her up when she passed the entrance to the house.

'For a walk!' Lucy looked up into his face and revealed her dislike. 'I suddenly find I need the fresh air!'

His expression was grim. 'Lucy, you don't understand!'

'I understand the hate, the violence!' She shook her head. 'You're just the same! Just like Paul!' She saw Alex's eyes narrow in a frown, but the words were said and she couldn't take them back. 'I need some space,' she added shakily, 'some time to myself.' She glanced beyond Alex's shoulder. Jeff was strolling towards them both, looking subdued. 'I thought that you were different, that underneath you understood.'

'I do! More than you know.' Alex's voice was low and wonderfully compelling, but Lucy knew that she couldn't give in. If she did ... she'd suffer.

'You spoke to me with such ...' Lucy searched for the right word ' ... such contempt. As if I didn't matter.'

'That's not true!' He was close. She could feel the brush of his thigh against hers, was achingly aware of the warmth and strength of his body just inches from her own. Alex took her by the arm, but somehow she found the strength to shrug free from his hold. 'You don't understand,' he grated. Smouldering dark eyes bit into her pale face. 'I asked you to trust me, Lucy—remember?'

'Oh, I remember all right!' she replied unsteadily. 'It was all part of the patter, wasn't it? You turned it on like a tap and expected me to go with the flow! Well, I'm not that easy, despite what Charles may have told you!'

'Charles told me nothing of any consequence.'

Lucy's expression revealed dislike. 'Don't lie!'

'Go, then!' Alex stepped away from her as Jeff approached. 'If that's what you want.' His voice was cold suddenly. 'As you've repeatedly reminded me, I'm not your keeper. I have no hold over you.' He turned, said something low and menacing to Jeff which Lucy couldn't catch and then disappeared without a backward glance into the house.

'Forget Alex,' Jeff drawled, strolling up to her. 'He's a tricky customer. I'm surprised so many women find him attractive.'

'They do?'

'Haven't you noticed? Females seem to like the mean, moody approach.'

'He's a very stubborn, arrogant man,' Lucy delivered flatly.

'Ain't that just the truth?' Jeff's mouth widened into an attractive smile. 'But there's no need for it to spoil our association.'

'He hates you,' Lucy murmured.

'Looks like it!' Jeff shrugged. Even white teeth gleamed in the evening light.

'You don't care?'

'Why should I?' Jeff began strolling down the track, away from the house. 'Do you love him?' He glanced sideways as Lucy caught up with him.

'No!' Had she replied too quickly? Lucy breathed in. 'He just makes me mad.'

'You didn't look too mad when you were dancing together.'

'I know.' Lucy bit her lip to stop herself from crying. 'But that was just dancing, wasn't it? It didn't mean anything.'

'Did you want it to?'

Lucy shook her head and Jeff continued easily, 'You know, you're different from other young actresses I meet. They're always on the look-out for a lucky break, always pressing, but you...' He paused and Lucy paused with him, debating whether to turn around and go back. She didn't have a clue where she was going, what she was doing with this man. The past fifteen minutes seemed to have passed by in a blur.

Jeff glanced back towards the house. They had covered a fair distance. 'Hasn't anyone ever told you to grab an opportunity when it arises?'

'What opportunity?' Lucy turned to look at him, but his gaze was fixed on Alex's villa, where light glowed from every window.

'I'm a director.' He smiled. 'I've been searching for a girl with your qualities ever since I took on this film,' he informed her smoothly, 'and up to now my search has been in vain.'

Lucy frowned. 'My...qualities? I wasn't aware I had any.'

He threw her a look. 'Is that what being with Alex does for you?' Jeff enquired. 'Kills all your self-confidence? He's written the book that this film is based on. There's a part you'd be perfect for and he's never mentioned it?' Jeff shook his head. 'Crazy. Well, *I* think you'd be perfect for it and that's what matters. Helena. She's a sort of magical apparition, a figment of a tortured man's imagination.'

'*Me?*' Lucy shook her head in a gesture of amazement. 'You can't be serious. You really do want to cast me in the role?'

'Why not?' Jeff's mouth widened and she saw the glint of white teeth and a huge chunk of charm in one dazzling smile. 'Doesn't the idea of pursuing your career appeal, then?'

'My career? But I just went to stage school for a couple of years. I never was very good...' She shook her head again. 'You're having a joke, aren't you?' she murmured. 'You don't really mean it—'

'I mean it.' Jeff kept his gaze hooked on her face. 'You'd be perfect. Do you want to give it a try?'

'I...' Her voice trailed to a halt. 'I don't have a clue what to say.'

'Say yes!' Jeff paused a moment. 'Unless, that is, you're frightened of what Alex might do. He'll undoubtedly forbid it.'

'Yes...' Lucy thought of his cold, hard anger, of the way he had spoken to Jeff. 'Yes, he will.' Then she remembered how he had spoken to her, how proprietorial his voice had sounded. As if he owned her. 'Well, he can forbid all he likes,' she replied shakily. 'He doesn't own me.'

'Good girl! That's what I like to hear—fighting spirit!' Jeff's smile showed his approval. 'Come along tomorrow morning.' He reached into his denim pocket and pulled out a scrap of paper and a pencil. Lucy watched him write, wondering what she was getting herself into. 'The address of the location. It's not too far.' He held the paper out to her. 'As it's most doubtful that Alex will offer to be your chauffeur, I suggest you go to the village and hire a taxi. I'll pay for it at the other end. I'd get someone to come and get you if I could, but time is tight and it's going to be all hands on deck in the morning.'

She inhaled a deep breath, reached out and accepted what she hoped was the first solid evidence of a new beginning. 'Thanks.'

'Now, don't be late!' Jeff's mouth curved teasingly. 'I'm nothing if not a hard taskmaster!' He reached forward and touched her cheek with a gentle finger. 'And don't look so worried; this will be the best move you've ever made, believe me.'

'I hope so.'

'I know so!' Jeff's smile broadened and charm oozed out from every pore again. 'What are you going to do now? You can walk with me. My car's parked just around this next bend. We could go and get a drink somewhere—'

'No.' Lucy shook her head quickly. 'No...thanks. I'd better be getting back. I need to do some thinking, and I know of a peaceful place where I can do that.'

'Don't let him talk you out of it, now!' Jeff smiled as he walked away. 'You have talent; anyone can see that!'

Except Alex, Lucy thought.

She felt cold suddenly. She hugged her arms around her thin silk dress and began to walk back, thinking of Alex, of his anger, and of her own foolish attraction towards him.

CHAPTER FIVE

THE party seemed to be moving up another gear. Guests spilled from the house onto the terrace and further afield, into the orchard and beyond.

Lucy slipped around the side of the house to the vegetable garden. She closed the heavy wooden door behind her with relief. It was still early but she wasn't capable of being sociable. She would stay here until everyone had gone home, then slip up to her room.

The garden was a blessed sanctuary. It wasn't particularly large, but it was lush with every sort of vegetable imaginable, all fighting for air and space, tumbling over one another in their desire to make the most of the sun and the warm Mediterranean rain. It wasn't just a confusion of leaf and fruit, there was order in this jungle too: well-used tools, stacked tidily against a wall, a mossy circle of grass with a bench nearby where the gardener could rest after a hard day's work.

She sat down heavily on the bench. She wanted to feel pleased and excited about the opportunity that Jeff had given to her, but she couldn't. Alex would be angry. He wouldn't let her do it. Her hands clenched into fists at her sides. She felt so dreadfully tight inside, so full of tension.

Oh, but come on! A small voice wailed in her head. Alex doesn't own you; he can't *order* you not to do something. What are you getting so worked up about? This is *your* life, *your* opportunity!

The door to the garden squeaked opened and Lucy moved restlessly on the bench, looking for another way out. She wasn't in party mood; she didn't think she could endure being sociable, or seeing anyone else being sociable either.

She got to her feet and glanced towards the door. A glimpse of dark hair. The sharp contrast of white shirt. That was all it took to make her heart pound like a stream train.

Alex strolled purposefully towards her. He looked sharp and cool and totally in control. Lucy spun away, frantically scanning the garden for another way out. She didn't think she had the strength to endure another bout of hostility, but unless she was prepared to dive headlong amongst the peas and beans she didn't see how she could avoid this next confrontation—for confrontation it would be. She could sense that the anger hadn't disappeared—the masked expression, visible as Alex came near, told her that.

'I looked every place else. I should have come here first.'

His voice kept her fixed to the spot. She couldn't help it. Everything about him was magnetic, like a force you simply couldn't ignore. She watched as he glanced around, his dark eyes flicking over the verdant scene. 'I had forgotten how restful this part of the garden is.' He stood a moment, saying nothing, just gazing, and then his eyes returned to her taut expression and she saw the flints of steel in their dark depths. His mouth was firm and incredibly hard. 'Are you calmer now?'

Lucy raised an enquiring brow. 'Calmer?' she repeated frostily. Was he goading her deliberately? she wondered.

She looked into the strong, handsome face, felt the by now familiar surge of attraction deep in the pit of her stomach, and found that she didn't have a clue what he was thinking.

She didn't know him; that was the problem. She didn't understand the way his mind worked, or what he was planning, or how he felt. She didn't understand anything.

'I'm fine!' she announced coolly. 'But if you don't mind I'd like to be by myself.'

'Perhaps I do mind.' He *was* goading her. Alex's mouth twisted into a chilling smile. 'Perhaps I mind very much.'

Lucy swallowed. 'Look, you've found me. I haven't run away or thrown myself off the nearest hillside, so you can enjoy the rest of your party in peace.'

The dark head shook a little. 'You think it's as simple as that?'

She threw him a cool look. 'Why shouldn't it be? I'm nothing to you.'

The cold look was accepted, increased two-fold and thrown back; icicles frosted each precisely spoken word. 'Maybe not,' Alex replied in clipped tones, 'but Charles has entrusted your welfare to me and you mean something to him.'

'May I remind you, Mr Darcy,' Lucy retorted sharply, 'that I am a grown woman with a mind of my own? I have to stand on my own two feet some time. Wasn't that one of the sermons you preached when I first arrived? Well, it's happening and it's happening now!' She paused, colouring a little at her strident tone. She could hardly believe that she was saying all this. 'I may have been less able to take charge of my life recently,' she continued determinedly, 'but, thanks to your particular brand of support—'

'Jeff and I go back a long way. There are reasons for my acting the way that I did.'

'Are there?' Lucy looked at him stonily. 'Well, I don't want to know them! He...he thinks I would be good in this film he's making.' She lost her courage and turned away from Alex. 'Your film.'

'You *are* kidding, I presume?' His voice held derision and a certain weariness, as if he couldn't quite bring himself to believe what Lucy had said to be the truth. 'You *are* just saying all this to wind me up?'

'Why should I do that?' She gave Alex the opportunity to reply but he chose not to answer. 'He seemed perfectly genuine.'

'Lucy, let me tell you now—you are no judge of people. Haven't your recent difficulties revealed that much?'

'I liked him!' Did she? Lucy wasn't entirely sure. All she knew was that she wouldn't have Alex talking to her as if she were an idiot.

'You're not going to do it.' Alex's voice was grim. 'I won't allow you to make a fool of yourself.'

'You won't allow me…?' She spun around, and stared at Alex in amazement. 'Well, that's extremely noble of you but I think I can manage my own affairs!'

'Like you managed your marriage?'

She felt the pain of his retort like a physical blow. 'You are such a…' she gasped.

He exhaled heavily. 'I'm sorry.' Fingers dragged glossy dark hair away from his face. 'I shouldn't have said that. I didn't mean—'

'Oh, yes, you did!' She spoke with hate in her eyes. 'You meant every word! You always do!'

'No, I don't.' Alex's tone was flat.

'You have no hold on me, no right to tell me what to do.'

'You're not having anything to do with that film!' He fixed her with hard, dark eyes. 'Is that clear?'

'I'll do as I damn well please!' Lucy retorted tempestuously. 'Just try and stop me!'

'If you accept a role in Jeff's film, you will regret it, believe me.' Alex's voice was quiet, assured and fully controlled and Lucy hated him for it. 'Which role has he offered you? The part of Helena?'

'Yes. And isn't it just as much *your* film?' she snapped irritably. 'It's based on one of your books. And anyway, why should I regret it? What harm can it possibly do to accept an opportunity which hundreds—no, thousands of girls would give their eye-teeth for?' Emerald eyes flashed and sparked a challenge. 'Are you telling me Jeff's not a reputable director? Is that it?'

'He's had his successes,' Alex snapped. 'Many people believe he's got a great future ahead of him.'

'But not you?'

'What I think clearly doesn't make a great deal of difference, does it?' he remarked stonily. 'You've made that much clear.'

'This is your film; I don't see why—'

'For goodness' sake, will you stop saying that?' he replied tersely. 'It's no such thing!'

Lucy frowned. 'But I thought you wrote it.'

'And that would make a difference, would it?' He shook his head in derisive irritation. 'It just goes to show how little you know about the film industry.' He threw her a vexed look, as if he didn't want to go to the trouble to explain but felt he had to. 'I wrote the book years ago, when I first started out. Since the screenplay will have changed it out of all recognition—' he released an impatient breath '—it's not mine any more.'

Lucy lifted her shoulders in a small shrug. 'So?'

'So, see sense! Forget all about this ridiculous idea. You're chasing rainbows.'

'I won't!' Lucy pursed her lips angrily. She felt lost and confused, but she was trying so hard to be strong. 'Why should I?' she cried. 'And may I remind you that I wasn't chasing anything? Jeff came to me. He offered me this chance because he thinks I've got what it takes. OK, so you don't feel the film's yours any more. Well, I didn't accept Jeff's offer because of that, so it makes no difference to me. I accepted it because it could be the start of something new—something fresh and true and good. It's an opportunity!' Lucy sighed and closed her eyes briefly. 'Goodness knows I've thrown enough of those away in the past.' Her lashes flew open and she looked up at Alex almost imploringly. 'Can't you understand? I want to make the most of this one.'

'You're living in a dream world.' He threw back her attempt to make him understand in her face. 'Can't you just accept my word when I say that this won't be the new start you're hoping for? You're not Michelle Pfeiffer and Jeff certainly isn't the new Steven Spielberg!'

'And you'd know, would you?' She threw him a look that showed hate. 'Well, thanks for your vote of confidence, but I don't need you telling me what I can and cannot do! Now if you'll excuse me...'

She spun away but Alex caught hold of her. Lucy glanced down swiftly, saw the contrast of tanned fingers against the paler skin of her bare arm, felt the heat of his touch. 'You're not going anywhere until you agree to scrap this ridiculous idea,' he gritted.

'Let me go!' Lucy frowned and tried to shake his hand from her arm, but he was too strong for her.

'Not until you see sense.' Smouldering dark eyes bit into her face.

'Never!' She backed away, pulling against his hold, but Alex didn't give in. 'You can't *make* me do what you want!' she cried. 'You can't treat me like some sort of...of possession!'

'Can't I?' Alex tugged her close. She was aware of the line of his thigh, strong and hard and muscular, pressing against her own, felt the firmness of his hand on her back, relentless and commanding, was conscious, even through her own anger, of the thrill of excitement as his fingers moved from her arm to the bare skin at her shoulder. 'Well, we'll just have to see about that, won't we?'

She was so wrapped up in his touch that she didn't recognise the danger in his words until it was too late.

His mouth descended with ruthless sensuality. His lips moved hungrily, demanding a response, demanding submission, and Lucy forgot how to think, how to move or breathe. She had been kissed before, but never like this. This kiss had an element of punishment about it, an erotic, relentless pressure that swept the angry tension away and replaced it with an intense physical longing.

She had never known such sensations. Her short time
as a miserable married woman had never prepared her
for this complex mix of emotions.

Alex's tongue parted her lips insistently. She felt the
ache of desire as he explored the outline of her body
with searching hands. His fingers curved over the rise
of her breast, slipping effortlessly across the smoothness
of the silk, outlining the dark peak which stood proud
and erect beneath the flimsy layers of bra and dress.

Lucy felt as if she was in a trance. She couldn't even
begin to analyse what was happening—whether it was
right or wrong, good or bad. She just knew she felt incredible, like a woman with a dream that was about to
come true, that *was* coming true.

'We shouldn't be fighting, not when we can be doing
this.' Alex breathed the words erotically against Lucy's
neck. 'Surely you can see that?'

His mouth plundered hers again and Lucy couldn't
reply in words, only in deeds. She gripped at his shirt,
running her hand along his neck, roaming her fingers
through the glossy black hair, pulling him closer to her,
increasing the pressure of their bodies as they clung
together in a timeless, frantic embrace.

Alex Darcy had her in his power, and with each second
that passed she felt herself losing control. She was in-
toxicated with overwhelming desire. At that moment
nothing else mattered—not the film, not their argu-
ments, not her past, not even her future. All she could
think of was how wonderful it felt to be in this man's
arms.

He lifted her easily, and with barely a pause in the
fluency of his lovemaking Lucy found herself lying on
the soft circle of grass. She opened her eyes dreamily,
caught a glimpse of starlit sky beyond Alex's shoulder,
switched her gaze to his face and found herself touching
the angled jaw, the firm outline of his mouth as if she
could hardly believe he was real.

'Alex . . . I—'

'Ssh.' His mouth hovered enticingly over her lips. 'Hell! You are so beautiful,' he growled.

'I am?' Lucy frowned uncertainly. 'You really think so?'

Alex captured her mouth time after time with his. She could taste him and it was wonderful. 'You have a charm, a sweet uncertainty that is wonderfully appealing,' he murmured distractedly. His mouth moved downwards to her neck. She shivered as his tongue trailed an enticing path. 'For God's sake, Lucy, why do you think Jeff wants you in his film?' Alex groaned urgently. *'Why?'*

Understanding dawned instantly. She froze beneath his powerful frame. She tried to sit up, tried to push him away with clenched fists, but he was too strong. She heard a pitiful cry and found that it had come from her own throat. 'How could you?' He raised himself up a little to look at her and she saw his frown, the firming of his mouth, the narrowing of his calculating eyes. 'You think I'm so stupid, don't you?' she croaked. She was panting, out of breath, feeling as if she had sprinted and sprinted and had got nowhere.

She knew! She understood! Alex Darcy had miscalculated and he didn't like it.

'Lucy? What the hell—?'

'Well, maybe I am stupid to let things get so far,' she cried, 'but at least I've woken up now!' She didn't want to look at him any more; she couldn't bear the humiliation of it—knowing that she had been so close to giving herself to a man who could be so cold and calculating. 'Let me up!' she spat. 'Do as I say or I'll scream!'

He moved from her and Lucy twisted away, scrambling on hands and knees to put distance between herself and Alex—the man who thought he only had to seduce her to turn her into a malleable puppet.

'What's got into you?' His voice was low. Dark eyes transfixed her face with their tight scrutiny.

'I've seen sense, that's all,' she replied shakily. She got to her feet, smoothing her crumpled dress down with trembling hands.

'Lucy?' Alex rose too, making a move towards her, but Lucy backed away as if his proximity caused her physical pain.

'Don't touch me! Don't you dare!' She hated the sound of her own voice, but there was precious little she could do about it.

Alex hated the piercing tone too; she could see that. He moved from her and a look of stony indifference replaced the mystified look in his eyes. 'You seem to imagine...' He raised his hands in an impatient gesture. 'The fact is that I have no idea what you think I am supposed to be guilty of, but, whatever it is, believe me...' jet-black eyes dared her to say otherwise '...you are mistaken.'

'Am I? Well, it doesn't seem that way to me.' Lucy gulped a breath. 'You want me to do what you want? Well, I won't do it, no matter how much of a hold you think you have over me.'

His eyes darkened with exasperation. 'I cannot believe I'm hearing this. You honestly imagine I would go to such lengths just to get my own way? Are you crazy?'

She saw instantly that he regretted his last choice of word, and that made her all the more angry. It was just a figure of speech, she knew that; he hadn't meant it in a literal sense, but in her present state of mind Lucy was unwilling to let it drop.

'Who knows?' she shot back. 'Having fallen so easily for your transparent seduction routine, I'm inclined to think that I should be back in the hospital receiving some sort of treatment.' Her hands flew to her head in a theatrical gesture. 'Maybe they could remove my brain. It doesn't seem to be serving me particularly well!'

'Thinking had nothing to do with what just occurred between us,' Alex asserted evenly. 'It was all feeling. You must know that. I didn't plan or calculate what might happen when I walked in here to find you.'

Lucy inhaled a deep breath. Her eyes stung with unshed tears but she looked him straight in the face. 'I don't believe you,' she said flatly. 'Men! You're all the same! I should have learned my lesson with Paul. He took what he wanted and didn't give a damn for anyone else's feelings—'

'I'm not Paul,' he gritted. 'You're overreacting.'

'I'm overreacting! I'm crazy!' Lucy's voice was trembling badly now, but she refused to allow Alex to talk her round. If he touched her again... She shut her eyes tight. 'I don't want to listen to anything you have to say,' she croaked.

There was a tense silence. In the distance the sounds of the party could be heard.

'In that case there's nothing else for me to say, is there?' She felt the chill of Alex's gaze and shivered. 'I'll leave you,' he added crisply. 'If you want to make a fool of yourself then that is your business. But don't come running to me when you find yourself in over your head!'

She watched him go. When the door to the garden was firmly shut, Lucy sank to her knees on the soft grass and burst into floods of tears.

She felt sick with nerves the next morning, but determined. Very determined. All through the night she had thought about it, and now that the sun was up she wasn't going to change her mind. She would walk into the village, get a taxi and find the location that Jeff had indicated on the piece of paper.

She thrust the address into the pocket of her denim shorts. She didn't have a clue what to wear—not that she had a great deal to choose from. She glanced in the mirror as she slipped on a loose mint-green shirt over a strappy white T-shirt to protect her freckled skin from the sun. She looked passable. Fresh and clean and healthy. Not stunningly attractive, she thought, not glamorous, but OK.

Pulling out a brush from her bag, Lucy ran it through her hair. She had decided to let it fall free. It shone in the early-morning sunlight, tumbling in gorgeous shades of gold and bronze more than halfway down her back, curling and twisting this way and that. Maybe she looked better than OK, she decided, eyeing her reflection critically; maybe she should allow herself to believe what Jeff had said about her being perfect.

It was quiet in the house. She couldn't face breakfast, so she took a selection of fruit from the bowl in the kitchen and placed it in her canvas bag for consumption later, glancing around at the mess of glasses and dirty plates strewn over every surface, not envying Maria the task of clearing up when she came later that morning.

She crept out of the house. It was still early—probably far too early for Jeff and the film, but Lucy didn't care. She had to get out. The thought of seeing Alex again after the misery of last night made her stomach churn.

She had seen him on her way to her room some time after midnight—drink in hand, laughing and chatting to a group of friends, all of them clearly having a very good time. Their eyes had met, but only for a second, then Alex had looked away, dismissing her, dismissing what had taken place between them . . .

She knew where the village was. They had passed it on the way from the airport. It was a fair walk, but if she kept up a steady pace she should reach it within the hour.

She ran the first few hundred yards, anxious that Alex might wake and spot her from his bedroom window. If she was lucky, he would tumble straight from his bed into the shower and then lock himself away in his study for the whole of the day. Lucy had taken the precaution of keeping her bedroom curtains closed and had shut her door, so if he did bother to wonder where she was before settling down to work he would hopefully assume that she was still asleep and not bother to disturb her. That was the idea, anyway.

She forced herself to concentrate on her surroundings. The countryside of northern Majorca was beautiful: green mountains, lush with vegetation; grey rocks; blue skies; pretty whitewashed villages clinging to the hillsides far away in the distance. Lucy rounded each fresh bend in the dusty track and found new delights at every turn. It was so quiet and peaceful too—an area where the pace of life surely hadn't changed in a hundred years?

Lucy heard an engine behind her in the distance. She had paused to eat some of the fruit that she had secured earlier. She dived into her bag for a handkerchief to wipe her sticky hands and stood back, as far off the side of the road as possible. A couple of old trucks had passed her since she had begun her walk and she had learned quickly that it was wise to stand well out of the way; otherwise she risked the possibility of an accident on the narrow, curving route into the village.

This time, however, it wasn't a truck. Lucy glanced back along the track, recognising the maroon Jaguar instantly for what it was—for *who* it was. She clenched the handkerchief into a ball and glanced about her for a hiding place, but apart from throwing herself off the edge of the hillside there was precious little she could do to escape detection.

She watched nervously as the vehicle made its way along the track, throwing up clouds of dust in its wake.

Alex's vehicle.

The car came to a halt alongside her. An electronic window slid down noiselessly. Dark eyes captured her face, rooting her to the spot. He spoke. 'I think you'd better get in.'

'No.' Lucy shook her head. 'No,' she repeated quietly. 'I'm going to the village to get a taxi.'

He looked sleek and formidable—assured, despite the fact that his denim shirt had clearly been thrown on

without a great deal of care. He hadn't even bothered
to do it up. She glanced at the row of metal fasteners
hanging loosely against the bronzed chest. Sculptured
pectoral muscles glinted in the sun; she glimpsed the flat
abdominals lower down—the hard ridges which indicated that he took care of his physique—and felt the
ache of desire, like a curse over her body.

'You really are determined to go through with this,
aren't you?'

'Yes.' Her reply was little more than a croak.

'I'll take you.'

'What?' Lucy didn't bother to hide her surprise. 'To
the village?' She wished her heart wasn't thumping so
loudly; she could hardly hear herself speak.

Alex released an impatient breath. 'I won't have you
walking alone along empty lanes. It's not safe. You
should have woken me this morning, instead of creeping
out of the house like a fugitive! What on earth were you
thinking of?'

'Last night!' she replied stonily. 'Your anger. Your
determination that I shouldn't go through with this.'

Alex regarded her with brooding irritation. 'It's still
there. Get in.'

'No.'

The door opened and he got out to stand before her.
He was close. Too close. She could smell the scent of
his shower gel, could see the last vestiges of water clinging
to the strands of glossy jet-black hair. 'Get in,' he repeated mildly, 'or be put in. It's your choice.'

Lucy took a step backwards and found herself up
against a tree. Alex's shirt swung open and she caught
sight of his bare chest in all its masculine glory.
'You...you can't make me go with you,' she stuttered.
'I know what will happen; as soon as I get inside that
car you'll turn it right round and head back to the house.'
She glared up at him. 'I won't have it! I've made my
decision and I'm sticking with it.'

'So I gathered when I woke up this morning and discovered you had gone,' Alex replied briskly. 'I'm not interested in an argument this early in the morning, Lucy, so you can take that frantic look off your face. Get in. I'll take you wherever you want to go.'

'You will?'

'That's what I just said.' Cool eyes rested on her face. 'What's the matter? Don't you believe me?'

'I . . . I thought you were going to stop me. I thought you didn't want me to have anything to do with this film.'

'I don't.' His tone was terse, as formidable as his expression. 'But what I want clearly makes no difference—'

'You're right, it doesn't!' she cut in swiftly. 'Don't worry about me; I can walk. It's a pleasant day and the village isn't too far away now, so—'

'You've misunderstood.' Alex walked round to the passenger door and opened it, staring at Lucy across the roof of the car. 'I drive you or you don't go anywhere. Now get in the car!'

'But—'

'I said, Get in!' His eyes dared her to disobey. 'Don't push it!' he warned. 'Just do as I say and be thankful that I'm capable of keeping my temper at this time of the morning!'

She would have been a fool to argue any further. Lucy wasn't quite sure what Alex would have done, but she was positive that she would have ended up the loser.

She walked round, sat inside the car, which smelt of leather and Alex's cologne, fastened her seat belt and sat in stony silence as he thrust the car into gear and drove with assured speed along the twisting, dusty road.

'Presumably you know where the location is?' Lucy enquired after ten minutes had passed, during which time the atmosphere had become so thick that it could have been cut with a knife.

'Yes.'

'Have you been there before?' she persisted, deter-mined not to be put off by Alex's clipped replies or the firmness of his jaw—unshaven, she noticed, and all the more attractive for that...

'Yes.'

Lucy released a taut breath. 'Is that all you can say?' she demanded.

'It's all I feel like saying,' Alex replied bitingly. 'Don't push your luck, Lucy,' he warned. 'I'm taking you, but that's as far as it goes. I should be home in my study, working. You should be lying around resting, recuper-ating. Not getting yourself mixed up with—'

'I don't want to hear!' she retorted, glancing out of the side-window, trying to admire the view. 'I know how you feel about it! You made that abundantly clear last night. You tried to change my mind both with words and actions and you failed. End of story.'

Alex looked across at her. She could feel his eyes boring into the back of her head, but she refused to turn and meet his gaze. She wouldn't put herself through that torture now. It would only remind her of last night, of how wonderful it had felt to be in his arms, how close she had come to allowing Alex to make love to her...

'You're so mixed up you can't see straight!' he gritted.

'And you can, I suppose?'

He didn't bother to reply. When he next spoke it was only to tell her that they had arrived.

Alex pulled the car to a halt and she stared dubiously through the windscreen.

There was a great deal of activity. The tranquillity of the area had been marred by lorries and trucks and masses of electrical equipment—huge lights, black snakes of cable that curved this way and that.

Lucy felt her stomach crawl with apprehension. Doubt overwhelmed her. She glanced sideways and saw that Alex was watching her.

'If you're having second thoughts, I can easily turn the car around. It's not too late... It will never be too late,' he informed her steadily, 'to change your mind.'

Lucy forced steel into her voice. 'I want to do it.'

He released a breath and opened the car door, his expression grim. 'As you wish.'

She got out and stood on legs that felt like jelly. Her gaze was drawn to the busiest area of activity, which centred around the huge catering truck away to their right. A line of people was queueing up outside and there were white plastic chairs and tables arranged at intervals, around which were seated many people, all of them, if seemed, tucking into huge platefuls of steaming food.

Jeff appeared from the mayhem. His multicoloured shirt was different from the one last night but equally loud. 'Great! You've made it!' He reached forward and kissed Lucy warmly on the cheek. 'You look fabulous!'

She smiled nervously, slamming the car door shut, glancing across at Alex as he emerged looking predictably unmoved by Jeff's effusive display of charm.

'Alex.' Jeff nodded a curt greeting that was in stark contrast to the welcome he had given Lucy. 'I must say I'm surprised to see you here.'

'Surprised or disappointed?' Alex enquired smoothly. 'I wasn't impressed with your idea that Lucy should walk into the village. It *was* your idea, I presume?'

'Yeah!' Jeff met Alex's challenging gaze. 'Why not? It's a great morning and Lucy didn't object to the idea last night, did you?'

'Whether Lucy objected or not is immaterial,' Alex replied curtly. '*I* minded.'

'You staying or going?' Jeff glanced across at Alex. 'Aren't you on the wrong side of a deadline?'

'If I am, it's no business of yours,' Alex replied with deceptive mildness. Enigmatic eyes scoured Jeff's face. 'I'll stay. Someone needs to be around to make sure Lucy's not taken advantage of.'

'That's the very last thing on my mind!' Jeff said easily.

'Is it?' Alex thrust his hands into the pockets of his denim jeans, his eyes narrowing contemptuously. 'I wonder.'

'I don't want you to stay!' Lucy's voice was brittle with nerves. She looked across at Alex. 'I'm quite capable of coping by myself.'

'Really?' He sounded almost incredulous.

Lucy felt anger rise. 'Yes!' she retorted. 'I am! And if you don't like—'

An insistent bleep came from the interior of the Jaguar just at that moment, preventing Lucy from finishing her defiant speech. Alex pressed his lips together in irritation and reached inside for the car phone.

Jeff diverted Lucy's attention. 'Come on over and I'll get you a coffee. Do you want some breakfast? One of the great things about location work is the great food that's in constant supply.'

'Er...no, thanks.' Lucy looked at Jeff, but she was acutely aware of Alex talking quietly into the mouthpiece. Alex looked concerned. 'I...I don't tend to eat this early in the morning.' She flicked her eyes away from Jeff's face and concentrated on Alex. 'Thanks anyway.'

'That was Maria.' Alex replaced the car phone, ignored Jeff and spoke exclusively to Lucy. 'Her elderly father has had a fall. They need someone to get him to hospital. Me.'

Lucy frowned. 'Is he all right?'

Alex shrugged. 'I've got no idea. Maria sounded extremely upset. She doesn't usually panic over trifles.'

'But what about the doctor?' Lucy enquired. 'What's happened to him? Or the emergency services?'

'The family doctor's out on another call. They can't get in touch with him. And, as for an ambulance— it would take too long. My car will be quicker. I'll have to go.'

'Don't let us hold you up.' Jeff threw Alex a cold look and then gestured to the catering truck. 'Go over and get yourself a coffee, Lucy; I'll be with you in a minute.'

'Lucy!' Alex thrust out an arm as she passed by.

'I'll be fine,' she replied firmly, determined to shrug off the little-girl-lost tag. 'I don't need your constant care and attention.'

'Oh, but I think you do.' Alex's gaze was hard and without relief. 'I don't want to leave you here.'

'You've got to help Maria. Please go!' Lucy worked hard at keeping her voice level. She hated the way that he was acting as if she were a child of ten or something. 'I really would prefer it if you left me to sort this thing out on my own. I'm not a child.'

Alex looked at her, eyes as cold as ice, lines of grim disapproval marking his handsome face. 'I'll be back as soon as I can.'

He walked towards the car. Lucy waited for a look, a last acknowledgement, but there was none.

Alex simply opened the door, got in and drove away.

CHAPTER SIX

LUCY stood in the shadows, straining her ears for the sound of Jeff's voice announcing her cue. In the sunlight the crew were waiting for her to make her move. She closed her eyes, cursing her own naïve stupidity. She wasn't prepared and Jeff knew it—they all knew it. He had taken advantage of her inexperience and was using it unmercifully.

You should have listened to Alex! You should have listened to him! The words reverberated around her head, tormenting her. He had known—or if he hadn't known he had guessed.

'OK, Lucy? Ready. And action!'

She didn't have to do a lot this time—just walk, just appear. She was an apparition, a ghost-like goddess figure emerging from the pretty wooden glade. Remember the camera! she told herself. Just do as Jeff told you. The sooner you get it right, the quicker you can get out of this dreadful costume!

'Costume' was overstating it. The outfit Lucy wore was barely more than a couple of metres of white voile draped elegantly over her body. She glanced down at herself and grimaced. The sun was shining, the lights were positioned with studied accuracy—she had the overriding suspicion that she might just as well have been walking through the long grass naked.

The third take. Were they doing it on purpose, she wondered, just to make her feel more self-conscious than she already did? Oh, stop it! she told herself irritably. Now you're being paranoid! These people aren't voyeurs, they're professionals. It's just a job to them, just a job...

If Alex were here... A surge of panic ran through Lucy's body at the very thought. She could see the imagined scene in her mind—humiliation, disgust, a look that told her exactly what he thought of her... Oh, hell! What on earth had got into her?

It was a blessing that he wasn't here. That was the only good thing about it. She had sent him away, pretended she was able to cope with all this. Fooling them both. Or did Alex know? Fully aware that she was on her own, had he left Lucy here to make her own mistakes, to discover all by herself what a naïve fool she really was?

'Cut! One more time!' Jeff came towards her as the rest of the crew relaxed from their positions. Lucy fixed her gaze on the psychedelic patterns of his shirt. She found she couldn't look him in the face.

'Now that was good, sweetheart, but not quite good enough, I'm afraid,' he informed her briskly. 'Your expression wasn't quite what I wanted; you seemed to have your mind on other things and you were a bit too fast with the walk. Try and look more purposeful. Remember what I said: you're a vision, the woman of Harry's dreams—'

'Jeff... I'm not sure I can go through with this.' Lucy inhaled a steadying breath. 'I feel so... so exposed!'

'Nonsense! You look wonderful.' Jeff's tone continued to be brisk and businesslike, although Lucy noticed that his eyes covered her body in swift appraisal. 'Of course you can do it! You look perfect. This is the beginning of a great career!' He began to back away. 'Now get back to your starting position and we'll try one more time. Remember,' he added over his shoulder, 'slow and purposeful!'

'So, how was it? Or am I not allowed to ask?'

Lucy slid into the seat and fastened her belt with relief.

She had felt like crying the minute Alex's long, immaculate car had come into view. He had looked so wonderfully strong and determined sitting behind the wheel. So solid. He had opened the door and got out,

leaning nonchalantly against the car with his arm resting
on the roof, looking for her with that dark, penetrating
gaze. It had taken all of her restraint not to run across
from the catering truck and throw herself into his arms.

She glanced across at him now, registering the
brooding gaze of enquiry, wondering if she were capable
of pulling this immensely difficult piece of acting off.
'Fine!' She smiled casually and busied herself, rooting
around in her bag for nothing in particular so that he
wouldn't be able to see the glaze of tears in her eyes.

'You enjoyed it, then?'

'Yes!' Lucy kept her head down. Her fair fell like a
curtain around her face, screening her from Alex's penetrating eyes.

'You must be tired.' He started the engine and thrust
the car into gear, casually resting his arm across the back
of her seat as he looked behind to reverse onto the road.
'Jeff kept you a long time.'

'There were a few problems with the light.' Lucy felt
the brush of his hand on her neck as he gripped the back
of her seat. She swallowed. 'And then there was something in the camera. It meant we had to do quite a few
things again.' She shrugged and pretended that it hadn't
affected her unduly. 'I expected a lot of waiting around.'
She inhaled a steadying breath. 'How was Maria's father?
You've been away a long time.'

'Miss me, did you?' Dark eyes looked scornfully at
her face. 'He's fine. A bruised hip. Nothing too serious.'
They were driving along the road now. Lucy kept her
eyes fixed on the lush hillside which spread away to her
left. 'What about you? How did you get on?'

'Oh, you know. . .' She kept her voice as casual as she
could. 'I think I'll have a swim when we get back,' she
added swiftly. 'It's been very hot today, hasn't it?'

'You don't want to talk about it.' Alex's voice was
grim as they rounded another bend in the road. He thrust
the car savagely into a lower gear. 'I wonder why?'

'Alex, please...' Lucy's voice almost broke. She pursed her lips together, debating how she should handle this. She knew one thing: there was no way she could tell him the truth. She had fought him too hard over this to sit back now, to break down in floods of tears like an inadequate fool. That would be the worst kind of humiliation. 'Look—' she released a tense breath '—I'm tired, OK? You were right about that at least. I...I just want to get back and relax.'

'Was I right about anything else?'

'What is this—an inquisition?' Lucy rounded on him, eyes blazing. Using her anger to shield herself was the only defence she had left. 'I had a great day!' she continued fiercely. 'Everyone was very friendly, very helpful. Jeff said I did a brilliant job! I'll probably be nominated for an Oscar!' She flashed him another angry look. 'There! Satisfied?'

'Do you expect me to be?' Smouldering dark eyes penetrated her flushed face. 'OK, I'll drop the subject. It's clear I'm not going to get a straight answer from you now. Maybe I'll call Jeff myself,' he added grimly, 'and ask how you went on.'

'There's no need for that!' Lucy's voice was sharp. 'I told you, everything was fine. I had a brilliant day.'

'Yes, and look up there!' Alex drawled, glancing up through the car's windscreen. 'Isn't that a pig I see flying across the sky?'

She scrambled from the car the minute they arrived back at the villa. She stood, toe tapping, waiting impatiently at the front door, fingers gripping the bag hanging at her side so hard that her knuckles were white.

'You look tense.'

'Is it any wonder,' Lucy retorted, eyes flashing, 'after all your questioning?'

'Do you feel all right?'

'Perfect!' she snapped. 'Just perfect.'

He threw her a dark look and her eyes fell hastily from his face. She couldn't keep this up. Her shoulders sagged under the weight of the day and her own confusing emotions. It was crazy. She desperately needed to be on her own, but a great part of her longed to be held by Alex. She had endured so much today. Oh, how she had needed this man's strength, his protection! I'm weak, she thought. So dreadfully weak...

Lucy inhaled deeply and made an almighty effort to appear relaxed, aware that it would sap the very last vestige of her strength. She took a step closer to the door. 'Could you open it, please?' she said with an attempt at calm civility. 'I really am desperate for a shower and a change of clothes.'

Slowly he inserted the key into the lock. 'I phoned Charles today, to tell him about your new-found acting career.'

'You did what?' Too sharp. Lucy watched anxiously as Alex looked back over his shoulder at her.

'He needed to know!'

'And I suppose you made it clear that you were dead against it?' Her tone was harsh and scathing. She found she couldn't help it.

'I told him I didn't think it was the best decision you could have made,' he drawled, 'but that you were determined—'

'What did Charles say?'

'Not a great deal.' He lifted his shoulders slightly. 'He was busy.'

'Of course.' Lucy shook her head, narrowing her green eyes as she looked up at Alex. 'How disappointing for you!'

'Meaning?' His voice was cutting.

'Well, I'm sure you had hoped for a more positive response,' she replied feverishly. 'Something equalling your own unreasonable anger, perhaps? You see, the trouble with Charles,' Lucy added, her tone rich with sarcasm, 'is he has an annoying habit of inconsistency— all one moment, nothing the next.' Her mouth twisted into a bitter smile. 'He had probably forgotten I was even staying with you.'

'Don't talk nonsense.' Alex opened the door. The cool interior looked inviting, like a sanctuary. 'Actually, Charles did start to talk about coming over to see you,' he continued unemotionally, 'but I persuaded him that it was time you were left to stand on your own two feet.'

'Oh!'

Dark brows were raised. Lucy had the sneaking suspicion that Alex was testing her. 'You sound surprised, or disappointed. It's what you wanted, isn't it?'

'Yes! Yes, of course it is!' She stepped across the threshold.

He moved in front of her, blocking her path momentarily. 'You don't look too sure. If you want to phone him back and—'

'I'm sure!' Lucy smoothed damp tendrils of hair back from her face with a shaking hand. 'Stop pressuring me, will you?'

'You think that's what I'm doing?'

'Yes!' She glared up at him. 'And I don't like it. OK?'

She ran around his huge frame and clattered up the wooden stairs, racing along the passageway to her bedroom. She slammed the door shut behind her and leant against it, trembling as if with cold or fright, feeling mixed up and alone and totally unable to cope.

The whole day had been a nightmare. She should have listened to Alex. She should have trusted his judgement, instead of throwing it all back in his face. Why did she have to be so stubborn? Stubbornness had got her mixed up with Paul. It had kept her with him long after sense had told her to make a swift escape. She should have learned. She *wanted* to learn.

But to tell Alex now, to admit that she had made a mistake? The prospect was not a pleasant one. In fact it was so unpleasant that it was unthinkable. He thought little enough of her as it was, and he had treated her badly; she couldn't forget what had happened between them last night.

Lucy closed her eyes as if in pain. She hadn't forgotten it. The pictures were too vivid, the sensations as real as if she were in his arms again, feeling his touch, his mouth, understanding the urgency, the need that had been simmering since she had first set eyes on him...

Lucy shook her head. It had all been a sham. Just a way of using her, manipulating her... I don't want to be a failure any more, she thought. I've messed my life up too badly already.

She thrust herself away from the door, pulled open a drawer and grabbed a towel. She had just removed the last of her clothes and was about to walk through into the adjoining shower room when there was a knock on the door. Lucy stared at her discarded clothes in dismay and then swiftly wrapped the towel that she was holding around her body. 'Yes?'

'Can I come in?'

'Er... hang on.' She glanced in the full-length mirror. The towel wasn't exactly giant-sized; there was a lot of bare brown skin on display—probably too much, although not as much as had been showing for most of the day...

Lucy picked up her clothes from the floor and hurriedly stuffed them under a nearby cushion. She gripped the towel and opened the bedroom door cautiously. 'What is it?'

'Jeff's on the phone.' Alex was leaning against the doorjamb, looking down at her. 'Do you want to speak to him?'

'I... I'm just about to get under the shower.'

'So I see.' Dark eyes traversed her body in casual appraisal and Lucy felt herself tremble deep inside. 'You've caught the sun,' he drawled. 'Your shoulders are quite burned.'

'Are they?' She looked down, glancing to the left and right, pretending that she could cope with this latest onslaught to her senses. 'Oh, yes. I . . . I should have taken some sunblock.'

His reply was instant. 'Or kept your shirt on.'

Lucy inhaled a rigid breath. 'Yes.'

Dark eyes watched her face. 'Why didn't you?'

'I don't know.' She tried hard to look at ease. 'I just got warm and . . . and forgot about the strength of the sun.'

'I'll find you some cream.' Alex reached forward and placed a cool hand on each shoulder. He looked into her face and his expression was full of ruthless sensuality. 'Better?'

'Yes,' she whispered.

Neither of them moved. Lucy didn't have the energy or the inclination to retreat. Her pulse was going crazy. His hands felt wonderful—soothing her heated skin, his fingers lightly circling her shoulders in a lazy sort of way, stimulating her warm brown flesh, controlling her mind and her thoughts.

How could it be like this? she wondered. How? There was no sense to it. No reason . . .

'Tell me about today.' Alex's voice was deep and even, but there was menace in his tone, an inclination towards savagery that could not be mistaken.

Lucy heard it and stepped away, backing into her room. She gasped and tried to appear calm. 'There's . . . there's really nothing to tell,' she said, with an attempt at lightness. 'It's pretty mundane.'

'I like mundane.' Alex took a step towards her into the bedroom. 'It has a quality about it that I find particularly reassuring.'

'Look, Jeff's on the phone.' Lucy moistened her drying lips with the tip of her tongue. 'I'd better speak to him.'

'Why?' Alex's eyes narrowed dangerously. 'The man's a creep. Surely you've worked that much out by now?'

'Look—' she turned angrily toward Alex '—I don't know what it is between the two of you, but your disagreements have nothing to do with me!'

'What did he do to you?'

Lucy flushed. Her fingers gripped the pink towel tightly around her body. 'Don't be ridiculous!' she said feverishly. 'He didn't *do* anything!'

'You think I'm blind?' Alex shook his head in angry disbelief. 'You think I couldn't see how tense you were when I picked you up?'

'I told you,' she repeated stonily, 'I was tired. It had been a long day—'

'Oh, spare me the excuses!' His expression revealed his contempt. 'They're an insult to my intelligence! What's he done—changed the role from ghostly apparition to sexy siren?'

Lucy hung her head. 'Something like that,' she replied miserably.

'I'll kill him!'

'No!' She frowned, looking anxiously up into Alex's face. 'Please! Leave it. It wasn't so bad—'

'You really expect me to believe that?' he gritted.

'I just felt conspicuous, that's all. Unsure of myself. I'll know better next time. I'll go and speak to Jeff,' she added somewhat wearily. She tried to move past him, but he blocked her path effectively with his towering frame.

'You'd be wasting your time,' he informed her. 'I told Jeff you were busy.'

'But you said—'

'I know what I said,' Alex replied evenly. He challenged her with his gaze. 'I lied. I wanted to see your response—it was much as I expected. You don't want to speak to Jeff any more than I do.'

'Games!' Lucy almost spat the word out. 'I might have known! Just like last night. That's all you're capable of—'

'Last night?'

Had he forgotten? Lucy felt the blow of humiliation. 'You know!' She didn't attempt to keep the vibrancy from her voice. 'In the garden!'

Deep dark eyes narrowed. 'If you're referring to our lovemaking—'

'Our *what*?' Lucy shook her head. Her lips parted in a tortured smile.

Why had she brought the subject up? Why? She kept her eyes on Alex's face, daring him to dispute what she was about to say. 'Don't insult me by pretending,' she muttered. 'There was precious little love connected with it. Power—that's what it was all about. A typical male who feels he has to assert his authority!'

'That's what you think?'

'It's what I know!' Lucy spun away towards the shower room. She didn't trust herself to look into Alex's face. 'Don't try and kid me into believing anything else, because you'll be wasting your time!' she added shakily. She wrenched open the door and was almost blinded by the dazzling white tiles which covered two thirds of the room. She held a suddenly aching head in one hand. 'Now if you don't mind I'd like to have my shower in peace.'

'And if Jeff calls back?' Alex enquired tersely.

'Then of course...' Lucy glanced briefly back at Alex '...I'll speak to him.'

'Of course.' His mouth curved with cool precision. It was a deadly smile. 'Tell me something.' He turned at the door to the bedroom as she struggled with her composure for a few seconds more. 'Why do you feel you have to prove yourself like this?'

Lucy's fingers slackened their hold on the towel and it slipped a little, revealing the curve of her smooth, full breasts. 'I...I don't,' she began. 'I just want to...to succeed.'

'Because you've failed up till now?' Alex shook his head. 'This isn't the way, Lucy, believe me,' he murmured. 'Not with this film. Not with Jeff. He's already made a fool of you, hasn't he? You're already regretting it. Another mistake in a long line of failures—that's what you were thinking when I picked you up this afternoon; that's what's going through your mind now. It's no good shaking your head,' he delivered quietly, 'I can see it in your eyes.'

His words released a trigger. Suddenly all of the tension and tiredness erupted and overflowed in one ferocious surge of feeling. 'Stop it!' Lucy flew at him, eyes blazing. 'You can't do this to me!' she cried. 'I won't allow it. I won't!' His chest was as solid as rock, but she pummelled it all the same. Her fists made little impression, but the ferocity of her attack, the sheer force behind her rage could not be ignored. 'So cool!' Lucy spat. 'You think you're so damned cool!' She stared up into the handsome face, hating him, hating the way he made her feel. 'How dare you presume to know me? How dare you?'

The towel slipped, edging down towards her midriff, but by now she was past caring. All she could think about was how little Alex cared, how low she had sunk to have such intense feelings for a man who treated her with such controlled indifference. 'I hate you!'

'No, you don't.' Alex didn't flinch from her blows. He stood impassively before her, taking everything she could give, waiting until the worst of her temper had blown itself away.

'Is that all you've got to say?' Lucy snapped. She gripped the front of Alex's shirt in irritated fury and tugged it sharply. 'Don't just stand there!' she sobbed. 'Say something! Can't you see what you're doing to me?'

For a moment she thought that Alex was going to turn away. He looked so rigid and inhuman standing before her, like a man who couldn't trust himself to move or speak. Then there was a change. His brow furrowed. His head shook a little as if there was no stopping the way he felt, or what he was about to do.

Lucy looked into his face and saw that the ebony eyes, which had appeared so cold and hard before, were melting into a smouldering mass of heat and fire.

Alex released a ragged breath. She could feel the force of it expelled from his body. It was as if he was getting rid of the restraints that had held him for so long. Then he gathered her in his arms, cradling her semi-naked body against his recently battered chest. 'I don't want us to fight,' he whispered huskily. 'I don't want you to hate me.'

'I hate myself,' Lucy croaked. 'I hate my life.'

'Don't say that.' He replied firmly. His hands were strong against her face. She closed her eyes, revelling in the pleasure of his touch. 'Do you know what you're doing to me?' he murmured huskily. 'Do you?'

His words mirrored Lucy's thoughts exactly. She swallowed the lump in her throat and wondered if Alex knew how desperately she wanted him to make love to her.

'I . . . I never meant to be like this,' she whispered.

'You've had a bad day.'

'I've had a bad few months.' She hesitated a moment then added, 'The day was a . . . strain.'

'I wish you'd taken my advice.' Alex tilted her face towards his. Mesmeric dark eyes contemplated her face. 'Why didn't you?'

Her brow furrowed into a frown. 'Don't lecture me again, please.'

'Is that what I do?' Alex released a tense breath; his dark head shook a little. 'I don't mean to.' His eyes lingered on her face. He lifted a finger and gently brushed away a teardrop from her cheek. 'You are so . . .' she watched as he searched for the word ' . . . sweet,' he declared softly. 'Sweeter than anyone I have ever known.'

'You make me sound like a little girl,' Lucy said quietly. 'I'm not. I'm a woman.'

'You think I don't know that?' Alex's voice held more than a hint of anguish. 'Charles has entrusted you to me—'

'I'm not his property!' Lucy murmured tautly. 'I've got a mind of my own.'

'And what is that mind telling you now?' Sensuous hands drifted up from the towel at her waist. 'What do you feel?' She gasped as Alex's strong fingers moved with slow purpose, brushing lightly against the curve of her breasts. 'You feel gorgeous,' he murmured huskily, cupping each full mound with unhurried ease.

Lucy forgot how to breathe. His touch annihilated all her doubts. A thrilling stillness settled over them and in that moment of mutual awareness everything was all right.

It didn't matter that the day had been a disaster, or that they had fought, that they *would* fight in the future. There was only this rush of sensation, this need between them that had to be assuaged...

He took his time. The dark eyes fixed to Lucy's face demanded attention. Alex wanted to see each reaction as his hands moved across her body. She yearned for his mouth, for the taste of him, and he gave it to her, but in small, succulent doses—warm, hungry kisses that left Lucy wanting more.

The four-poster bed beckoned. Alex lifted her effortlessly, and the cool linen sheets were soon caressing Lucy's heated body. 'If we do this...' he looked into her eyes as his determined hands trailed a path of delicious ecstasy '...I want there to be no doubts, no regrets.'

'Alex, please!' Lucy hardly recognised her own voice. She closed her eyes, her fiery hair splayed out like a halo against the soft pillows as she arched her half-naked body in silent offering. She needed this; she needed him...

The sounds from the outside world didn't seem important at first. The crunch of tyres on gravel, footsteps, even the faint ring of a bicycle bell didn't have any impact.

Alex's hands and body were the only things that mattered. His mouth covered hers, his tongue plundering the soft, sensual depths, inviting Lucy to do the same to his. She did, and for a long while their kiss was everything, full of hunger and passion, inciting their bodies into mutual need and desire.

Then kissing wasn't enough. Lucy's fingers searched for the buttons of Alex's shirt; she fumbled urgently as his mouth covered hers in total domination. She wanted to feel his warm bare skin against her own.

Alex brushed her fingers away and ripped open his shirt, tearing the buttons from the fabric without hesitation. He rose above her, shrugging the shirt from his shoulders, looking down with gleaming dark eyes at Lucy's naked breasts.

'So beautiful,' he murmured huskily. His fingers touched the dark peaks gently, moving slowly downwards, stroking the flat planes of her stomach, slipping beneath the edges of the pink towel, tracing the contours of her inner thigh, so that Lucy gasped aloud with the pleasure of his touch. 'If you knew how much I want you...' Alex's voice was rough with desire.

'Show me!' Lucy pleaded. 'I'm sick of the fighting and the lies.'

He looked tortured suddenly. Lucy stared up into Alex's stunning face and frowned. A breath caught in her throat. 'What's wrong?' she whispered. 'Alex, if you knew how much I wanted us to make love—'

'Lucy... there are things I need to tell you...' His fingers traced the outline of her face and his touch was gentle. His eyes were warm, his voice husky and full of the vibrancy that she had come to expect, but something was wrong and Lucy didn't know what it was.

'What things?'

She waited. He hesitated. Then came sounds that were too close to ignore—a loud knock at the door below, a female voice calling Alex's name.

Alex stiffened, listened as the voice repeated his name, and uttered a curse beneath his breath. 'It sounds like Maria.' His expression hadn't altered. His mind still seemed to be caught up with other things. Lucy clung to him for a moment, glancing anxiously up into his face. 'It's OK,' he murmured. 'Cover yourself up. I'll go and get rid of her.' He made a move, but Lucy reached out and caught his arm.

'Alex . . .' She shook her head, hardly knowing what to say.

He waited, frowning down at her, staring with eyes that no longer held the same degree of sensuous desire. 'I'll be back,' he told her softly. 'Wait for me.'

Lucy lay on the bed, rigidly clutching the towel around her body, and watched him leave the room. It wasn't going to be the same. Maria had ruined the moment. Or maybe, she thought, remembering the expression on Alex's face, it had been ruined before.

Insecurity cloaked her like a shroud. When she had been in Alex's arms everything had been all right. Now that he was no longer touching and kissing her she felt alone, unloved and desperately unsure. He had wanted her, that she couldn't deny—no one, surely, could fake such urgent need, such sexual desire? But then something had happened; something she had said or done had changed things.

Lucy turned on her side and pressed her face into the pillow. She waited. When she heard Maria and Alex laughing below she knew that there was no point in lying alone any longer.

'Lucy?' Alex looked surprised to see her. He turned as she emerged from the house, casting watchful eyes over her scantily clad frame.

'I thought I'd have a swim.' Her voice was brittle. She hugged the towel close around her swimsuit, smiling as best she could in Maria's direction.

'Maria's come all the way here on her bicycle at this hour of the day because she's worried about the fact that she missed work.' Alex shook his head and said something to Maria in Spanish. 'I told her there was no need to worry when I saw her this morning, but she felt guilty because of the mess from the party.'

'She's a good worker.' Lucy swallowed. 'You're lucky to have her.'

'Yes, I know.' Alex moved towards Lucy, and it took all of her powers of self-control not to stare at his gleaming, naked torso, at his denims slung low on his lean hips. 'Why have you come down?' he murmured, touching her shoulder, causing a thousand familiar sensations to shoot through the whole of her body. 'There was no need. I said—'

'I know what you said!' Lucy raised emerald eyes and stared up stonily into Alex's face. 'I just felt like a swim.'

Alex's eyes narrowed. 'We could swim together.'

Lucy said swiftly, 'I don't think so. Besides, you're going to take Maria back home, aren't you?'

Maria said something in Spanish and Alex answered her briefly. 'This is hellish bad timing, isn't it?' He looked across at Lucy's face and there was the torture again, just a brief glimpse of anguish in the taut dark features, but enough for her to know that things weren't going to come right even if Maria got on her bike and pedalled back home again.

'Take her!' Lucy insisted.

'You mind. I can see that,' Alex replied. 'You mind a lot. Hell! *I* mind!'

'No, I don't.' She kept her voice as casual as she could. 'The poor woman's not had the best of days, has she? And it's a fair ride back into the village. Of course you must take her.'

'Don't!' Alex caught Lucy by the arm. He looked angry suddenly. 'Don't play-act! Bad enough that you've been doing it all day.' He exhaled. 'Don't you understand?' he added sharply. 'I want the real reactions, the real you!'

'That's what you're getting!' Somehow she managed to maintain a calm look. She had gone too far along this particular road now to back down. She felt so angry with herself. The scene upstairs had developed out of passion and anger—mostly anger. Lucy couldn't risk basing any kind of relationship on that. She'd been hurt so badly by Paul, had pretended everything was right even when it wasn't... She couldn't judge people, that was the problem. Paul, Jeff, Alex. Each of them in their own particular way had only wanted to use her.

Lucy managed a careless smile. It almost cracked her face. 'We got...carried away. It's best that Maria...' She struggled to find the words. 'That she interrupted us.'

'You don't believe that for one moment!' The words were flung at her harshly.

'What's wrong with you? Why can't you accept things as they are? As I want them to be?' Lucy hissed. She stepped away from him, conscious of Maria only a few feet away. 'I'm going for a swim!' she announced flatly.

'We'll talk when I return.' Alex's eyes travelled the length of her body. She could feel the power in his gaze. 'I won't be long. Fifteen minutes at the most.'

It wasn't a threat or a piece of information to be taken lightly; it was a promise.

'Take as long as you want,' Lucy replied shakily. She gave up pretending. The intolerable ache that she felt deep inside couldn't be ignored any longer. She inhaled a deep, steadying breath. 'I...I'll be in bed—asleep,' she added hastily, 'when you get back.'

'And if I decide to wake you up?' Alex's powerful gaze tested all of Lucy's resolve. 'What then?'

CHAPTER SEVEN

LUCY heard the Jaguar as it roared away and looked across to see an angry cloud of dust flying up in its wake. If Alex keeps that speed up, then by journey's end, she thought, Maria will be wishing she had stuck with her rusty, battered old bike.

She dropped her towel onto a nearby bench and thought of plump, sedate Maria clinging to her leather seat as Alex unintentionally frightened the life out of her. He would look grim and intense, his jaw set into the firm line that she knew so well.

She closed her eyes. They had been so close to making love. How had it happened so fast? One moment they had been fighting, the next...

Don't think, she told herself. Don't feel. Forget this ache inside; it will go away in time. You've done the right thing. You know you have.

Did she? It didn't feel particularly right. She felt as if she'd just made the biggest mistake of her life.

Lucy climbed down the steps and slid into the pool. She closed her eyes and swam below the surface. If she had been feeling good, if everything had been right between her and Alex, then she could have appreciated the gorgeous setting.

The sun was at that wonderful stage, burning orange in the evening sky, spilling golden rays onto the shimmering surface of the pool. Ahead lay the endless greenery of the valley. And somewhere, driving along a narrow, winding road, was Alex.

Lucy surfaced and swam up and down the large pool for several lengths without pausing, concentrating on her strokes, trying to block out everything except the feeling of her limbs slicing cleanly and gracefully through the still blue water. She craved exhaustion. If she was that tired, she wouldn't have the strength to dwell on the physical desires that were still assailing her body.

Did Alex still feel it? she wondered helplessly. That need that had flared so fiercely between them? Was it all about sex? Just sex...?

She flipped over, floating aimlessly on her back, staring up at the evening sky, trying desperately hard not to think about the scene in the bedroom. Failing miserably. A few desolate tears trickled down her cheeks and merged with the water.

'Well, now, isn't this just a wonderful scene?'

Lucy heard the click of steel toecaps circling the edge of the pool. She tilted her head and watched as bleached denims strolled around the tiled perimeter. Her heart thudded. 'Jeff? What are you doing here?'

'I've come to see you.' He smiled and then crouched down on his haunches, watching Lucy in the middle of the water. 'Don't worry; I saw Alex leave.'

She couldn't help looking worried. 'He won't be long. He's just taken Maria, his housekeeper, back home.'

'Yeah, I saw them. He was driving like a demon.' There was a slight pause. 'Had a bust-up, have you?'

Lucy didn't answer. She laid her head back on the water, looking up at the first few stars. She couldn't help feeling slightly apprehensive and she didn't know why. Maybe it was because Jeff's timing was a little too perfect. The thought crossed her mind that he might have been waiting somewhere, watching...

'Alex designed this very well, didn't he?' Jeff stood up and looked about him. 'Quite enclosed and secluded, but great views.' There was a pause, presumably while Jeff admired the valley below, then the footsteps continued, slow and calculating. 'I'm pleased to see that you can swim.'

Lucy stiffened. She didn't want to swallow the bait, but curiosity got the better of her. There was something about his voice. She tilted forward and stood waist-deep in the middle of the pool, smoothing back the long, wet strands of hair from her face, staring suspiciously at Jeff, who still had the same amiable smile on his face, still chose to wear a shirt that was loud and tasteless—large swirls of violent red set against a mustard background. 'Oh?' She worked hard at keeping her voice casual. 'Why's that?'

'Didn't I tell you?' Jeff manufactured an artless expression. Lucy saw his gaze rest on her body. The swimsuit was close-fitting and it was wet. She hastily bent her legs and submerged the upper part of her body, ruining Jeff's view. She saw his mouth curve in amusement. 'I'm very keen to insert a swimming sequence into the film at some point. Fantasy for Harry. A bit like today's piece of filming—sort of dream-like.' His smile widened; there was a flash of perfect white teeth. 'Nothing to worry about.'

Her heart sank like a stone. Nothing to worry about? She thought of the actor who was playing Harry—a lecherous, good-looking sort who fancied himself rotten. She looked at Jeff, remembering her costume. It didn't take a great deal of intelligence to work out the sort of shots he had in mind.

'Why didn't you mention it today?' Lucy replied, trying to keep her voice level.

'It's no big deal. Besides,' he added casually, 'I didn't want to burden you with too much in one fell swoop.' There was a brief pause. 'You were good, by the way. I wanted to tell you that before you left, but you skipped off with Alex before I got the chance.'

'He was waiting for me. And . . . I felt tired. It was a long day.' Lucy flipped onto her back again, concentrating on a particularly bright early star that was visible in the rapidly darkening sky, refusing to allow her gaze to be drawn towards the side of the pool.

'You'll get used to it,' Jeff drawled. 'You've got great style.'

She forced a strong, clear voice. 'I'm not sure I want to.'

'What?' Jeff sounded as if he didn't think he'd heard properly.

Lucy inhaled. 'I don't think I'm up to it.' She swam over to the side of the pool where her towel was draped and pulled herself out. Jeff followed. He picked up the towel from the bench and handed it to her. 'It was nice of you to give me the chance and everything,' she added, drying herself awkwardly, 'but—'

'But Alex has put his foot down.' Jeff's tone was flat and sure.

'No, it's not that,' Lucy replied swiftly. 'I just feel that...that—'

'You forget,' Jeff delivered evenly, watching her with steady brown eyes, 'Alex and I go back a long way.' He shook his head impatiently. 'Of course this is all down to him! He's given you a hard time, hasn't he?'

'He doesn't like you. That isn't helping,' Lucy murmured.

'What is wrong with that man?' Jeff shook his head and threw Lucy a look of sympathy. 'So, Alex is ruining your career on the strength of our disagreement. Do you honestly think that's fair?'

'Fair?' She lifted her shoulders in a helpless shrug. 'I don't know.'

'He's got to you, hasn't he?' Jeff persisted. 'Turned the screw a little? Given you an ultimatum?'

'No... not really.' She shook her head miserably. She wished she could be strong. She felt as if she was being tugged both ways. What Alex wanted. What Jeff wanted. What did *she* want—really? 'Alex isn't happy about my acting in this film, you know that, but that's not the reason I'm having second thoughts.' She continued to dry herself. The towel wasn't as large as she would have liked; she could feel Jeff's gaze boring into her. 'I've had a... a difficult time recently,' she added awkwardly. 'Personal problems—'

'You and Alex?'

'No.' Lucy shook her head. Then she thought of the turmoil of feelings over the past couple of days and added, 'Well... not exactly...'

'Your relationship,' Jeff drawled. 'I'm having trouble pinning it down. Care to enlighten me?'

Lucy knew that she looked startled. 'I... I don't think it's any of your business,' she murmured. 'Besides—'

'Besides, Alex wouldn't like it!' Jeff finished evenly. 'Honey, he really does have a hold over you, doesn't he? Look, I don't want to sound cruel,' he added softly, 'but you really ought to be careful. Alex has a roving eye. He isn't the type of man to make a long-term commitment. I'm not saying it *will* happen, but you could be old news before too long, and then where will you be?' He touched her cheek softly, confusing her with this sudden display of kindness. 'Don't throw this chance of a career away,' he urged. 'You'll only live to regret it.'

He was right. She didn't want to admit it, but he was. Jeff had summed up everything so succinctly.

Oh, not about the film but about the man she loved. Jeff no more thought that Lucy was capable of holding Alex's attention than she did.

'Why did you fall out?' she asked suddenly.

Jeff took the question in his stride. She watched carefully for signs of discomfort or guilt but there wasn't any. 'Over a girl.' He threw her a crooked smile. 'Can you believe it? Alex can be extremely proprietorial at times. She chose me. He didn't like it. It was an ego thing, pure and simple.'

'Oh... I didn't imagine it would be anything like that.' Lucy's heart plummeted like a stone in a pool. She could scarcely believe it. 'He must have loved her very much,' she added quietly, trying to imagine what sort of a woman could cause such long-lived intensity of feeling.

'Oh, yes.' Jeff looked at her baldly. 'He did. *Very* much.'

She didn't want to dwell on that. She didn't want her imagination running riot, picturing scenes between Alex and some unknown woman—scenes that would tear her soul apart. 'I felt so...so exposed today,' Lucy confessed suddenly. 'I didn't like it.'

'You looked great,' he replied. 'Everyone thought so.'

'But this swimming sequence...' She looked at Jeff anxiously, still trying hard not to dwell on Alex's past love life. 'What will I wear?'

'Much the same as you have on now. Did you think...?' Jeff shook his head and grinned affably, suddenly more like the man she had met at the party. 'Lucy, I can see you're a girl with standards. I'd never expect you to do anything you're not comfortable with. If you weren't happy today, you should have said something.'

Jeff's gaze drifted a moment. He looked beyond her shoulder for a brief second and then warm, brown eyes focused on her face once more, reassuring her. 'There's no need to look so worried. Come here, you crazy girl,' he added suddenly, 'and give me a hug!'

Lucy frowned, hesitated, and then Jeff was enveloping her in his arms. She felt the strength of his sinewy frame as he held her close and knew that such contact with Alex would have resulted in total surrender, whilst this left her feeling startled and more than a little uncomfortable.

'I don't want you to worry about a thing!' Jeff released her, just as Lucy had decided to pull away, but he didn't retreat as far as she would have liked. 'You've got great potential,' he added smoothly. 'It would be a crime to throw it all away.' He smiled down at her and placed the flat of his hand against Lucy's cool cheek. 'You really have got a special talent,' he murmured.

And then, before she knew what was happening, he was lowering his head and his lips were parting in preparation for a kiss.

His mouth hardly made contact.

Lucy heard footsteps. Then a large, infinitely recognisable hand came into view and suddenly Jeff's body was being hauled roughly away.

She tried to say something—anything—but shock made the words stick in her throat. She watched in horror as Alex directed a blow to Jeff's jaw which sent him spinning backwards into the pool.

'What are you *doing*?' Her voice finally emerged as little more than a croak. She stared in disbelief at the pool, watching anxiously for Jeff's body to come to the surface. 'He might not be able to swim!'

'Good!' Alex looked across at her. Lucy saw the cold anger in the dark eyes and shivered. 'That will suit me very well,' he added savagely.

She held a hand to her head in a gesture that portrayed all of her amazement and shock. 'What on earth's got into you? Why did you have to hit him?'

'Are you being deliberately obtuse?' Alex's lips curled, but without humour. 'I always knew he was a fast worker,' he spat out in disgust. 'I didn't believe, though, that you could be such a fool!'

'Why? Because I happen to find him a more reasonable human being than you?' Lucy retorted sharply.

He came towards her, dragging her roughly by the arm. 'Even you can't be that naïve!' he thundered. 'Surely you don't think Jeff has cast you in this film because of your acting abilities?' The dark head shook in disbelief. 'Can't you see? He's using you, for Pete's sake!'

Emerald eyes flashed angrily. 'And you're not, I suppose?'

'We've had this conversation before.' Alex's voice was instantly crisp. 'It's becoming extremely boring.' He glanced towards the swimming pool. Jeff was making his way to the side. Alex looked at Lucy coldly. 'The creep's not going to drown. Satisfied?'

'Alex . . .' Lucy shook her head, hardly able to believe the way things were turning out. 'I didn't expect him to . . . to kiss me.'

'But he did.'

'It wasn't the way it looked!' she cried despairingly. 'If that's what's worrying you—'

'*Worrying* me?' His look of scathing disbelief was completely humiliating. Lucy knew that she had presumed too much and blushed scarlet. 'Save the explanations!' Alex added roughly. 'I saw all I needed to. You were a fool—and *I* was fool enough to allow that man to use you. Well, it's not going to happen again!'

Alex hauled Jeff bodily from the pool. Lucy closed her eyes, half expecting more violence, but miraculously there wasn't any. There were promises, though, uttered in steely tones by Alex, which obviously sank home, because when Lucy next opened her eyes Jeff was already walking across the terrace, muttering empty threats, dripping water as he went.

'He knows what will happen if he dares to show his face here again.' Alex followed Jeff's progress with cold, hard eyes.

'He talked about suing you for assault,' Lucy whispered anxiously. 'I heard him.'

'Let him!' Alex walked towards her, menacing intent in every line of his body. 'I'd enjoy the fight.' His fingers closed over her wrists. He tugged her close, then his hands were sliding around her waist and in the next moment he had lifted her clean off her feet.

'What do you think you're doing?' Lucy struggled in his arms on principle, although the sudden contact sent an intense and debilitating shock of desire through her veins. She would have loved to press her face against the crispness of his shirt, to wind her arms around his neck and sob uncontrollably against his chest. But she didn't. 'You can't treat me like this!' she croaked. 'I . . . I won't have it!'

'I can treat you any way I see fit. Charles has entrusted you to my care—remember?'

She was appalled. She stared into his face and saw that he meant what he said. 'You're acting like a...a madman! Where are you taking me?'

'Inside!' His voice was infinitely hard. 'You're cold!'

He was right. She was chilled inside and out. All Lucy wanted was a hot shower, a warm bed and to forget that any of this had ever happened.

Alex, however, had other ideas.

He barged open the door of her bedroom with his shoulder. Lucy was still in his arms...still struggling helplessly, still getting nowhere.

'What are you going to do?' she breathed as he laid her none too gently onto the bed.

His gaze drifted towards her body. Lucy watched as dark eyes surveyed the low-cut blue swimsuit. He approved. There was no mistaking such a look. The wet Lycra material clung to Lucy's firm breasts. She shivered and Alex reached forward, gathering the towel around her shoulders. He tugged her angrily towards him. 'I know what I would *like* to do!' he gritted.

'You...you can't!' Her eyes were wide with anxiety. The mood Alex was in at this moment, he looked as if he was capable of almost anything.

Alex transferred his gaze to the line of thigh, where skin and material met. Lucy's temperature rose. She felt exposed, as if she was kneeling naked before him. He wanted her to feel like this, she realised; he wanted her to remember the hunger of his gaze when there had been no material, no barriers between them.

'Jeff didn't do anything wrong!' Lucy spelt out tempestuously. 'In fact he was kind, understanding!' Alex shook his head in a derisive gesture and she added feverishly, 'I'm trying to make something of my life! Can't you understand that? You have a career, a future. What have I got?'

'Someone who cares for you.'

Lucy's stomach flipped a somersault. 'Who?' she whispered swiftly.

Alex was silent for a long moment and hope blossomed foolishly in her heart as the seconds passed and dark eyes rested impassively on her face. 'Who do you imagine? Charles, of course,' he delivered roughly. 'He wouldn't want you mixing with the likes of Jeff any more than I do.'

'You're doing this on purpose.' Lucy shook her head helplessly. 'You're wrecking my chances just because of some ridiculous disagreement over a girl.'

Alex's whole frame stilled. A dangerous silence settled between them. 'Jeff has been talking, I presume?' His voice was hard, his expression sharp.

Lucy gulped back the sob in her throat. 'He mentioned something, yes,' she mumbled.

'And you believed everything he told you?'

'Y-yes.' She looked into his rigid face. 'At least—'

'You believed him.' Alex said the words with a chilling lack of expression.

'Well, you tell me, then!' Lucy cried in desperation. 'Tell me what happened between the two of you! Tell me, and then I can understand!'

For a moment she thought that he was going to turn away, then a look of rigorous control settled over his features and he spoke quickly and without emphasis of any kind. 'He took away my sister. He used his charm and his money and his promises of a better life. And she fell for it.' There was a slight pause, then he continued. 'And then, when she was well and truly hooked, he told her he didn't want to see her any more.'

'Your *sister*?' Lucy shook her head. A quiver of remorse vibrated in her voice. 'I thought... Jeff mentioned a girl... I thought—'

'You thought what he wanted you to think! You looked up into those big brown eyes and swallowed every word!'

'You're not being fair!' Lucy gritted tightly. 'I had no reason to imagine he would lie about something so...so—'

'Important? Grow up, Lucy! I tried to tell you what sort of a man he is and you wouldn't listen! You're so damned naïve!' Lucy saw a glimpse of pain in the dark, smouldering eyes. 'Just like Carla.'

'Your sister?'

Lucy released a taut breath. 'Yes,' he replied flatly. 'My sister.'

They stood looking at one another for what seemed an endless moment. Finally Lucy found the courage to speak. 'You told me that you had no family,' she murmured. 'No ties to keep you in England.'

'She's dead.' He spoke the words firmly, the tone of his voice and the pain in his eyes defying further questions.

'Oh...I'm so sorry!' Lucy pressed her lips together to hold back her emotion. Alex looked so wonderful standing before her, so full of male vitality, so devastatingly handsome. So unhappy. More than anything she longed to take him in her arms and hold him tight. He knew about grief and the pain of losing someone. And she did too. But if Alex rejected her now she wouldn't be able to cope. He would destroy the small amount of self-esteem that she still had left—Paul had managed, even in the short time they had been together, to extinguish the rest.

Within the confines of the Lycra swimsuit, Lucy's body burned. She couldn't let him suffer alone. 'Let me make it better,' she whispered. 'Please!'

Alex looked down into her face. 'I was so angry before,' he grated. 'Seeing you with Jeff—'

'Forget Jeff!' she replied fervently. 'He's not important.'

'I know.' He stroked a damp tendril of hair back from her face. His hand shook a little. 'You're cold. You should get in the shower.'

Lucy swallowed with difficulty. This was going to be a moment to remember. This was going to be the moment when Lucy Harper finally found the courage to make the first move. She couldn't go on like this. She couldn't let Alex suffer behind that mask of agonised control any longer. 'When you hold me, everything feels right,' she whispered shyly. 'You must know that.'

'Yes.' His voice was husky with desire, but infuriatingly he made no move towards her.

Was he going to wait for her to ask? Lucy wondered. Did she have to *plead* for the pleasure of his touch?

'Alex...I...I can't go on like this,' she whispered tremulously. 'You must know...' She swallowed. 'You must know how I feel.'

'Lucy!' His voice held an edge of torment. The dark head shook, and for a moment she thought that Alex *was* rejecting her. But then his eyes were devouring her and she knew the torment had to do with some other, unknown situation. 'Are you sure you want this?' he asked huskily.

'More than anything.'

His dark eyes smouldered fire. 'If I touch you there'll be no turning back.'

'I know.'

'And if our relationship is just a brief encounter, what then? Could you cope?'

Lucy swallowed. He was forcing her to open her eyes to the reality of the situation. She should be grateful. 'If I have to,' she whispered.

'Lucy...I can't be everything you want me to be!' Alex asserted roughly. 'I'm never going to be your knight in shining armour.'

'You need me!' She asserted with surprising force. 'You want me! You know you do!' She pressed the palm of her hand hesitantly against his broad chest and found the thud of his heart. 'I can feel how much. I want to make you feel better,' she continued earnestly. 'I want to help you.'

'Dear Lucy!' It was a muttered exclamation which sounded more like a prayer, and then, with an anguished groan, Alex threw off the shackles of restraint.

Impatient, possessive hands held her damp body as if she were everything. His mouth was warm and urgent against her trembling lips, then his hands stripped off the swimsuit without preamble, revealing her nakedness beneath, so that his eyes could feast and revel in the sight of her smooth golden skin.

Strong, urgent fingers cupped each breast, moving with practised ease over each darkened nipple. Lucy lay proud, almost brazen before him. It felt good to be naked, to see Alex's dark eyes devour each full curve, each line. There was no doubt that he wanted her. No doubt that she wanted him. What was the use in pretending any longer?

He smiled. His gaze was rich with heat and passion. Lucy's heart flipped over as she basked in the warmth of it. And then he began to kiss her throat and her neck. His mouth dropped ever lower and Lucy forgot to breathe. 'I'm sick of fighting this,' he told her huskily. 'We've wasted too much time,' he murmured. 'Too many hours . . . whole days . . .'

'I know.' Her breasts rose and fell as the heat of desire overwhelmed her. Slowly his fingers drifted downwards, following a gentle path over her chin, down her throat, drawing an invisible line between the valley of her breasts. 'I need you!' he growled. 'I need you so much.' His mouth was urgent upon her lips, kissing with hunger and passion.

He pulled her closer and she felt the thrust of his tongue as his mouth plundered hers in erotic need—a prelude to the pinnacle of possession.

Then he sat upright, pausing a moment to take in every inch of her naked body. His shirt was removed with feverish haste, each button revealing a tantalising glimpse of bronzed torso. Then his fingers tackled the buckle of his belt and soon his trousers were consigned to the floor. He wore the sexiest briefs. Helplessly, Lucy found her eyes locked upon his body . . .

His first thrust was a glorious pleasure. Possession, power, total surrender...

Lucy clung to Alex as if her life depended on it. He was working the most incredible magic. She could feel the urgency within him, but he kept it under control, staring down into her face, reading the signals her body sent out.

Outside, the evening had changed to dark night. Inside the bedroom, shadows moved rhythmically, with regular intent. Lucy's hands roamed over Alex's broad back, gripping and twisting his smooth skin. She had never experienced anything even remotely like this. When had she ever felt this way? Not with Paul.

He was working the sort of magic that she had only dreamed about. Feeling him within her, feeling the muscles of his thighs as they flexed against her own, was pure ecstasy.

Whatever happened after this, however many things went wrong, she knew that she would never regret this moment. Never.

Afterwards, they lay together for a long while in silence, tangled limbs covered in a sheen of sweat, both replete, thinking their own thoughts, knowing that what they had just experienced was special.

'So, how was it for you?'

She looked towards him. She could see his strong profile in the darkened room, knew from the light, sensual tone of his voice that the attractive mouth was curved into a smile. She hesitated a moment, her eyes drawn towards the chiselled contours of his body, and considered all the adjectives that she could use to describe the wonderful way she felt inside. 'Different,' she whispered finally.

'That's a cautious reply.' Alex twisted onto his side and looked into her face. 'No regrets?'

She smiled and shook her head. 'No.'

'Good.' He kissed her softly on the mouth.

'You?' she asked hesitantly.

'Only that I fought this crazy situation for so long.' He stroked the edge of her cheek. He looked wonderful in the half-light: so strong and sure and full of male vitality. 'I've been so stupid,' he murmured, half to himself. 'Next time—'

'There is going to be a next time, then?' she queried softly. She moved closer to him, pressing her body against his.

'If you want there to be.' Alex's arm circled her waist, keeping her close. 'You are a very desirable woman; you must know that. Making love to you again will be as easy as breathing.'

Lucy's lips twisted into a smile. 'I breathe a lot,' she replied unsteadily.

Alex dropped a kiss onto her mouth. 'So do I.'

His hands began stroking her skin—a sensual rhythm that heightened all her senses.

'When I arrived,' she confessed daringly, 'I felt so...so frustrated and mixed-up. I wanted to hate you.'

'But you couldn't.'

'No.' She shook her head. She knew that he was smiling; she could see the gleam of even white teeth in the soft light.

'Good.' Alex's mouth brushed her lips again. 'Progress.'

'Alex..' Her eyes closed in pleasure as his hands continued to do delightful things to her body.

'Mmm?' He was preoccupied. His dark head lowered. Lucy shivered in delight as his mouth grazed her breasts, suckling the dark peaks erotically.

'I'm glad we've made love.' He moved her effortlessly into a new position, his hands still stroking and touching her skin. Lucy looked into the contours of his face and wished she had the courage to tell him how she really felt about him.

'So am I.'

Lucy smiled at his words. *She* had done this. She had changed Alex from aggressive tormentor to sensual lover.

She had helped him forget the pain of his sister's death. 'I can't believe that...this is happening,' she confessed hesitantly. 'After...the past few months...'

'Forget all that, for the moment at least,' Alex instructed her softly. 'Just concentrate on here and now. Do you like it when I do that?' he asked huskily.

His hands were like instruments of ecstasy, stroking and kneading her skin with practised ease. There was no doubting that Alex was an expert lover. The thought that many women had surely been subjected to such delights as she was experiencing now speared her mind, along with Jeff's words of wisdom.

She mustn't allow herself to begin fantasising about things that simply could not happen. Alex enjoyed living a solitary life. He enjoyed sex like a connoisseur. Deep, meaningful relationships were not on his agenda. And if they were—well, they would undoubtedly be with someone far more intelligent and sophisticated than she.

Telling Alex that she couldn't live without him and that she wanted to be at his side for ever and a day would not be the best move; Lucy knew that and accepted it.

'What's happened between us...it doesn't have to change things, does it?' she asked hesitantly.

'You mean you still want us to argue and fight?'

'No, no, of course not.' Lucy inhaled a steadying breath. She felt she needed to get things clear, make Alex see that she was capable of handling a casual, grown-up sort of relationship. 'What I mean is, I don't expect any sort of commitment,' she added awkwardly. 'I know you think I'm young and...and immature but I'm quite capable of—'

'Expect or want?'

'S-sorry?' She frowned. Alex was lying against her, his hands like electric shocks against her skin, still touching her, but not moving, not doing anything.

'You don't *want* commitment; is that what you're saying?'

Lucy hesitated. She wanted commitment from Alex so badly that she felt like crying. But this was undoubtedly a test; she could hear the sudden rigidness in his voice. 'I just want us to enjoy what we have,' she whispered. 'I don't want there to be any more...misunderstandings. I want to keep things simple,' she added firmly.

'I see.'

She wished that she could tell if he did, but the deep, even tone gave nothing away and the contours of his face were in shadow.

'But you do want us to continue...' there was a slight pause '...coming together like this every once in a while?'

'If you do,' Lucy murmured unsteadily. She placed her hand over his. 'I never imagined I could feel as good as this...'

'You've had a rough few months.' Alex exhaled and put some distance between them—just a fraction of space but it felt like a mile. 'In the heat of passion it slipped my mind. Your husband—'

'Don't talk about him—please!' she cut in swiftly. 'Not now.'

'Sorry. That was crass of me.' He sounded annoyed with himself. 'I talk about enjoying the moment and living in the present and then I bring up the one thing that gives you pain. If you regret—'

'I don't!' Lucy softened her voice. 'I told you. You've made me feel like I exist. For a long while I didn't know what I was doing, who I was, what I was supposed to feel.'

'And now you do?'

'Yes.'

Alex kissed her mouth and touched her intimately again, and Lucy felt the ache of wanting him as fiercely as ever. 'I didn't expect you to be like this,' he drawled huskily.

'You thought I'd cry and cling and generally make a fool of myself?'

He wasn't paying a great deal of attention. She gasped as his fingers seductively grazed her skin. 'Not exactly,' he replied distractedly.

'Strong, independent women are more your type, aren't they?' Lucy persisted.

'I suppose so.' His head lowered and his mouth traversed the flat planes of her stomach. The ache within her was pure ecstasy; watching Alex's seduction of her only served to heighten the pleasure.

'I'm not strong...' she murmured as the waves of desire began to grip her with all their force. Her mouth could hardly form the words. 'And I've... never been independent. What a pity you don't go for weak, pathetic women,' she panted after a long moment, 'who have a history of making all the wrong decisions—'

'Forget history,' Alex replied urgently. 'The future starts here.' He increased his efforts and Lucy arched her body in response as he positioned her hips at the juncture of his. He smiled—a slowly seductive, knowing smile that conjured up erotic images of master and slave. Then he took her with all the gritty determination of a man who knew what he wanted and had no difficulty in getting it.

Lucy gasped aloud. Before had been magical enough; this time the depth of feeling was beyond her wildest dreams. On and on, wave after wave of delectable, thrusting possession. Until the crescendo, the moment of glory, the point when stars burst and angels sang...

Afterwards—for a long while afterwards—they lay still. The night became an inky blackness. Lucy pressed her body close to Alex's strong frame in the darkness and closed her eyes. She felt the warmth of a coverlet being drawn around her body, and for the first time in a long, long while looked forward to tomorrow and slept—deeply, dreamlessly, happily.

CHAPTER EIGHT

THEY slept late. The sun streamed in at the window and
blinded Lucy when she opened her eyes. Alex was still
beside her looking incredible—tanned and powerful and
sleeping peacefully. All that she had ever wanted.

She moved cautiously at first, then with more
boldness, stretching her long legs luxuriously against his,
feeling the taut, hard power of his muscular limbs.

He awoke. Deep dark eyes fringed with luxuriant
lashes blinked once or twice and then crinkled as he
smiled. 'Good morning.' His voice was wonderfully
rough and gravelly. His jaw was shaded with the dark
stubble of beard. He reached forward and ran his fingers
through her tousled hair. 'How are you feeling?'

Lucy's mouth curved happily. 'Like a new woman.'

Alex surveyed her body with idle possessiveness, his
gaze lingering on the curves and lines of her naked torso.
'There wasn't much wrong with the old one,' he drawled.
'Nothing that a few sessions similar to the one we enjoyed last night couldn't cure, anyway.' He kissed her
mouth with slow sexuality. 'You weren't as inhibited as
I thought you'd be.'

She drew her head away a little and frowned into his
face. 'You thought I would be?'

Alex ignored the edge to her voice. He kissed her again,
but this time Lucy pulled away before the feelings of
desire could overwhelm her completely.

'What's the matter?' He exhaled a breath. It showed
signs of patience and that made her feel worse. Dark
eyes rested on her face. A gentle finger skimmed her
cheek. 'Look, I loved the fact that you were
so...so—'

144

'Willing?' Lucy swallowed and tried to keep her expression calm.

She felt hurt and she didn't really know why. Sexually everything had been just as she had dreamed. Alex had possessed her with all the power and passion she could have wished for. He had held her and caressed her, done all that a man could do to give the impression that he cared. She had no right to expect anything more.

And besides, Lucy told herself swiftly, words didn't mean a thing; actions were what counted. She only had to look back at her life to see that. Mothers might *say* that they loved you, but when they left you the truth was plain to see. And husbands could fool you with talk of togetherness and commitment, even as they were drinking and gambling and taking other women to the marital bed.

'Lucy, don't start putting words into my mouth,' Alex warned. 'All I'm saying is that you were relaxed, comfortable with yourself, with your own body. It was a wonderful surprise to find that you could make love with such abandon.'

'You mean considering that my husband has been dead for only two months?' Lucy replied stiltedly.

He made no reply. She saw his look, though, and knew that she had gone too far. Her hands reached for him, but he had flung back the bedcovers and got out of bed before her fingers could make contact with his warm brown skin. 'Alex, I'm sorry! I don't mean to be like this!' She frowned across at him, noting with despair the shuttered, hard expression that had been drawn across his face. 'I'm . . . I'm still mixed up.'

'I know.'

That didn't help. Lucy gulped back sudden tears and wondered if it was her destiny in life to go from happiness to desolation in such a short space of time. 'Where are you going?' she asked tremulously.

'To shower, then to my study.' He glanced back at her and his expression was still hard. 'I have a deadline to meet.'

'Alex, I didn't mean to—'

'Oh, yes, Lucy, you did. Why pretend?' He cursed and she flinched at the severity of it, at the look of rigid tension that shadowed his face. He inhaled a deep, steadying breath, shaking his head a little. 'Maybe last night was a big mistake. You are still trying to come to terms with your husband's death. How can either of us pretend otherwise? You need an easy, light, companionable sort of relationship. Something safe and steady. I'm not capable of giving anyone that—let alone you.'

'But you do still want me, don't you?'

'Of course I want you!' Alex's voice was as harsh as Lucy's was soft. 'I'm not a saint!'

'That's what you said to Charles on the phone,' Lucy whispered, frowning. She wrapped the sheet clumsily around herself and edged towards the bottom of the bed.

'I know.' Alex looked down at her. He was standing naked before her. Angry and naked. 'What he'll make of all this, I don't know!'

'It's none of his business!' she retorted. 'He's my stepbrother, not my keeper!'

'But he expected me to—' He stopped abruptly and shook his head. He searched Lucy's face and his expression softened a little. 'To look after you. To *help* you.'

'And so you have!' She clambered across the bed towards him. There had been something about his look that she didn't understand, but she brushed aside the doubts and clutched at his arm. 'Alex, I'm sorry about before. I don't know why I got so uptight! Please don't tell me you regret what's happened between us.'

'I don't regret it.' He looked down into her frantic face and kissed her gently on the mouth. 'Physical desire's a powerful thing. When it has us in its clutches there's precious little we can do about it.' He paused and then carried on speaking before she could protest further. 'Even the best of us are capable of saying and doing almost anything in moments of passion.'

Lucy frowned. A cold, desperate feeling began to claw at her heart. 'You?' she whispered.

Alex exhaled. 'Most definitely me.' He tried to smile, but it didn't quite come off. 'I told you, I'm not a saint.'

'I never expected you to be!' she replied quietly. She sighed and tried to be the sort of woman she imagined Alex wanted her to be. 'Do you want it to continue?' she murmured. 'Please say yes,' she added quickly. 'I won't cling. I won't cry. I won't have hysterics every time you look at another woman.'

He frowned. 'You really don't mind if our relationship is *that* casual?'

A coldness settled heavily inside her, but she valiantly ignored it and answered in the way she thought was best. 'No, I don't mind.' Did she sound convincing? She hoped so. 'Can't you understand?' she cried. 'Alex, you made me feel good last night. I'm a woman but I've been feeling like a child—acting like one. I need something good and positive to hold on to.' She gulped a breath and prepared to lay everything on the line. 'I...need...you,' she said, with slow emphasis.

Alex's hands fell to her bare shoulders. His grip was firm and warm. 'You *think* you need me—'

'I do!'

He looked down at her in silence for several agonising seconds. 'It's what you want?' he asked quietly. 'Really?' Lucy nodded and he added huskily, 'Making love to you will be no sacrifice. After last night you must know that. But—'

'It doesn't have to be complicated,' she replied swiftly, scared that he might be about to give her a list of the reasons why their relationship would be a mistake. 'I mean that.'

'Just two people, giving and taking physical pleasure,' Alex stated evenly.

'Yes.'

'You don't know me,' he murmured.

Lucy frowned, unsure of his tone. 'I know enough!'

He shook his head in disagreement. Then, without warning, his hands slid down from her shoulders to catch her wrists. Lucy gasped as he tugged her naked body towards him, positioning her hands against his bare loins in erotic command. 'You know this,' he murmured, looking down with fierce intent into her emerald eyes. 'Is it really enough?'

She opened her mouth to reply, but before she could answer, his lips were on hers and Alex was kissing her with a drowning, hungry need that left her senses reeling.

He worked for the rest of the day, but she didn't mind. The afterglow of making love lasted well into the afternoon and early evening. Alex had taken her with a passion that had dispelled all her fears. It had been a fierce, obsessive encounter that had left them both breathless and lost for words.

Lucy stretched her arms above her head and closed her eyes against the sun's evening rays. She was half-naked and she felt bold. Her skin was warm and tanned after a day of careful sunbathing.

Need stirred in her body. The afterglow was wearing off. She wanted Alex again.

He was still locked away in his study. Lucy could see the glow of his light from the terrace.

She hadn't made any attempt to interrupt him today. She knew better than that. His work was important, and besides, if she wanted to continue with her new image of calm, casual lover, then she had to keep her distance. It had been an effort, though, not to go knocking on his study door. Especially at lunchtime. She had half hoped that Alex would appear and eat with her, but he hadn't, so she had made do with a plateful of fruit and cheese on the terrace, stifling her disappointment as best she could, forcing herself to dwell only on the positive aspects of their relationship—on the way he made love to her as if she were the last and most desirable woman in the world.

She rose from the sun-lounger, pulled a flimsy blouse over her naked breasts, slipped her feet into her sandals and strolled across the terrace towards the house.

Alex's study door was ajar. Lucy pushed it open and saw that the room was empty. The computer screen was on, though, and Alex's desk was littered with paper and books. He couldn't be far away.

Cautiously, she took a step inside. The words on the screen fascinated her. She perched on the edge of his black leather chair and began to read a few lines of dialogue.

'What do you think you're doing?'

His voice made her jump. He sounded hard and un-friendly and she hadn't expected that. Lucy swivelled round on the chair, feeling as guilty as a child caught stealing candy. 'N-nothing!' She smiled and lifted her shoulders in a self-deprecatory shrug. So silly to feel this way. What harm could she possible be doing? 'I won-dered where you'd got to.'

'I was upstairs, looking for a book.' Alex had one in his hand. She glanced at it, but he deftly placed it on a shelf, out of reach, spine inwards so that she couldn't see the title. 'You shouldn't be in here.'

His abrupt tone made her frown. She'd thought that she had been mistaken before about the slightly ag-gressive voice. 'I wanted to see you,' she replied simply. 'You've been locked away in here for hours!'

'I have to get this finished.' He avoided her gaze. She watched as he gathered up the papers and books that were on the desk. 'I'll be out later.'

'How much later?'

'I don't know. As long as it takes.'

'You look tired.' Lucy watched as he thrust papers into the drawers of his desk. She could sense the tension in his body, see the rigid line of his expression. She desperately wanted to touch him, but common sense told her that this wasn't the time or the place. He had been working too long and he was clearly edgy. 'Why don't you have a rest?' she suggested evenly. 'Have you eaten? I could make you something.'

'Thanks, but no. If I want something I can get it myself.'

He had hardly looked at her, just a savage glance as he had entered the room. She was wearing a skimpy bikini bottom and a thin blouse that left little to the imagination, but she might as well have been dressed in thermal underwear for all the effect it had. Lucy struggled to keep the light tone in her voice. 'I'll make us something. It will be no trouble. We could eat out on the loggia, like we did on the first evening—'

'I told you, I have a hell of a lot of work to get through!' Alex cast her an irritable glance, which softened a little as he laid eyes upon her face. 'Lucy, I know you mean well, but you don't understand. This really isn't a good time for me—'

'Oh, I understand!' Her eyes flashed angrily. She stood up and faced him. 'Don't worry, I understand only too well!' She walked towards the door on legs that felt like jelly. 'You're an important man with important work to do. I was forgetting. Silly of me!'

He caught hold of her just as she was about to slam the door shut. Large, commanding hands gripped her around the waist and dragged her against the hardness of his body. 'You don't understand at all,' he growled. 'Not a thing. Not one damned thing!'

He kissed her softly when she had been expecting strength. He spoke to her in harsh, almost anguished tones, yet she could see, *feel* that he was sorry. 'I can be such a swine,' he murmured huskily, his mouth

moving erotically against the softness of her neck.
'Forgive me.'

'I do.' His hands were roaming her body. She would
have forgiven him anything at that moment—anything
at all . . .

'You feel warm.' His fingers explored confidently,
moving beneath the flimsy material of her blouse to hold
and caress the fullness of her breasts. 'I've had to fight
so hard to keep myself locked away in here.'

'Surely you've done enough?' Lucy whispered, shiv-
ering as he moved against her, gasping as his strong
fingers roamed her body with passionate intent.

'Enough?' He smiled seductively and kissed her hard
on the mouth. She felt the thrust of his tongue, the
strength of his need and revelled in the glow of their
mutual desire. 'I don't think so, do you?'

Alex manoeuvred her back against the wall, positioning her with ease. 'We'll eat later,' he drawled.
'Afterwards.'

He took her there and then, understanding the needs
of them both better than Lucy had anticipated. Swift
and sure, with sensual, almost savage undertones, their
union released all of the tension that had built up during
the day.

Afterwards he held her and touched her with gentle
reverence, looking into her eyes, kissing her face many
times over.

'Do you believe I'm sorry now?' He drew her blouse
together, dressing her, fastening each tiny button as if
she were a little child.

She smiled up into his ruggedly handsome face. 'Of
course,' she whispered.

'I need a long, hot bath before dinner—care to join
me?'

'More than anything,' she said, smiling up into his
face. She stroked a strand of dark hair back from his
eyes and kissed him softly on the mouth. She liked these
moments almost as much as making love. This was when

she felt close to him, when she secretly felt that there was a chance of something meaningful and long-lasting happening between them.

He lifted her effortlessly and carried her up the winding stairs. Lucy hadn't seen Alex's room before, and although it was a little more cluttered than she had expected it was not unlike the way she had imagined it to be. It had strong, simple lines, with splashes of Mediterranean colour here and there in the form of cushions and curtains and one or two well-chosen pictures which hung strikingly on the whitewashed walls.

Lucy twisted her head around towards the bed as Alex walked through to the *en suite* bathroom. 'You'll see it later,' he informed her. 'We'll sleep here tonight.'

A glow of pleasure wrapped itself around her body. If this was Alex's idea of a casual relationship, then she wasn't about to complain.

It was dark and she couldn't sleep. She didn't know why, because she was relaxed and certainly tired enough.

A clock chimed the hour. Lucy counted two strokes. It was later than she had imagined. A familiar pain gnawed at her stomach. She felt hungry; that was why she couldn't settle.

She twisted on her side to look at Alex. She loved the way he looked when he was asleep. So relaxed. A man with the worries of the world lifted temporarily from his shoulders. He looked so strained and tense a great deal of the time. Why was that? The pressure of his work—was that the reason? Lucy brushed a finger gently against his naked shoulder and released a small sigh. I don't know him, she thought. I don't know anything about him. But I love him—more than he'll ever know.

She folded back the bedcovers and slipped out of bed.

Staring into the dark and thinking realistic or even unrealistic thoughts was painful as well as pointless. Lucy knew how things stood. She had gone into her re-

lationship with Alex with her eyes open. He had made
it plain enough how things had to stand between them.

She slipped on a robe and hugged it against her naked
body. The towelling fibres were imbued with the lingering
scent of Alex's cologne and she pressed the sleeve against
her face and breathed in deeply. Then she tiptoed out
of the room, only risking a light when she was at the
bottom of the stairs.

His study was as they had left it earlier—light blazing,
computer still on. Lucy went inside. She glanced at Alex's
desk, wondering if she should turn off the machine or
leave it for him to deal with in the morning. The latter,
most definitely, she decided swiftly. What did she know
about computers, anyway?

Lucy smiled happily and released a deep, contented
sigh. She felt so good, so needed. OK, so Alex didn't
love her, but he wanted her. That was more than
enough—for the moment at least.

She sat in the black leather chair and swivelled joy-
ously, feeling as light-headed as if she had been drinking
wine.

A photograph, high up on one of the shelves, caught
her eye. Lucy stopped turning and stared at the picture
for a moment before reaching for it.

She was lovely. Lucy held the frame in her hand as
her curious emerald eyes examined the happy, smiling
face. Carla?

She looked at it for a long while, mulling over the
things that Alex had told her. There were still aspects
she didn't fully understand. Jeff had treated Carla badly,
but was that fact alone really enough to account for the
force of Alex's anger?

Lucy didn't think so. She placed the photograph back
on the shelf thoughtfully.

Then she saw the book.

It was the one Alex had placed up there earlier. She
picked it up, turning it over in her hand. Presumably
Alex needed this for his writing. His work was still on

the computer screen and Lucy longed to look at it, but she felt it was the wrong thing to do, akin to prying. Maybe she would ask him outright if she could read his work later, but this book might give her a clue to the nature of the novel he was working on.

Lucy's heart thudded when she read the title, and that was silly because it looked like a perfectly boring book, not exciting or thrilling at all. *Psychology. The scientific study of the human mind and its functions*. She swallowed and told herself to stop overreacting. So Alex had a book like this on his shelf. So what?

Lucy flicked through the pages and then banged the book closed. There had been many similar books on the shelves of the psychiatrist who had treated her at the hospital. She released a breath. It was for research. Alex needed it for his writing. It was no big deal.

Lucy heard movement from the bedroom above. She listened as Alex's footsteps crossed the room and the stairs creaked under his tread.

No time to retreat now. She placed the book carefully back on the shelf and sat back down on the chair, swivelling gently to and fro. It would look silly if she scuttled along the passageway like a frightened rabbit. It would look as if she had something to hide...

A thought crossed her mind. Lucy pictured the way Alex had placed the book on the shelf. Did *he* have something to hide? She frowned and then with a concerted effort dismissed the thought as just another of her middle-of-the-night anxieties.

'What are you doing down here?' Alex's voice was gruff from recent sleep. He rubbed at his eyes and squinted in the light. 'Lucy?'

'I was feeling hungry. We never got around to eating—remember?'

'The kitchen's in the opposite direction,' he pointed out. 'What are you doing? I thought I told you that I preferred it if—'

'I know! I know!' She rose from the chair and walked towards Alex. He looked wonderful. Miles of bare brown flesh just waiting to be kissed. Lucy rested her hands lightly against his chest, standing on tiptoe to press her lips against his mouth. 'But I saw the light. Your computer's still on.'

'So it is.' He stepped around her, pressed a couple of buttons on the keyboard and then flicked a switch. The incessant humming of the machine stopped and the room became quiet. Alex looked down into Lucy's face. 'You haven't touched anything?'

'The chair!' she replied lightly. 'It's great for swivelling!'

'Nothing else?'

She hesitated a moment. 'The photograph. It caught my eye and I picked it up. Don't be cross!' she added swiftly.

Dark eyes scanned her face. 'You expect me to be?'

'She's very beautiful,' she replied, glancing back to the high shelf.

'Yes.'

'It *is* Carla?'

Alex nodded. He turned away from Lucy and the photograph. 'Shall we have a midnight feast?'

'You loved her very much, didn't you?' she whispered. 'But I don't understand everything.' She hesitated a moment and then decided to plunge in. 'Do you blame Jeff for her death?'

There was silence. Alex's mouth firmed into a hard line. Then he spoke in stilted tones. 'Yes. He treated her badly. She couldn't cope...' There was another long pause. Lucy waited, watching Alex's enigmatic expression, knowing that beneath the mask there was a man who felt the pain of loss. 'Carla drove her car off a cliff when she found out Jeff had been deceiving her.'

'Oh, Alex!' Lucy covered her mouth with one hand, her emerald eyes narrowing in horror as she looked up at him. 'I'm sorry,' she whispered. 'You loved her and she's dead, and I'm so very sorry!'

'I know.' He inhaled a steadying breath and drew her towards him. 'I don't want to speak about it any more—not with you,' he replied wearily. 'It's just more pain, and you've had enough of that to last a lifetime.'

'So have you,' she murmured. 'I wish you'd told me before.'

'When you first arrived?' He shook his head. 'Not then. Telling you anything at that time would have been supremely difficult.'

'Because I was so awful?'

His mouth twisted into an attractive smile. 'Partly. But you were feeling fragile too. The last thing you needed was to hear my problems.'

'I wish you had told me,' she murmured. 'I'm stronger than you think.'

'No, you're not.' Dark eyes held hers. 'Not yet. You need someone to take care of you.'

Lucy held her breath. 'Who?' she murmured finally. 'You?'

'Think of me as your guardian angel,' Alex drawled. 'Whilst you're here, I'll do my best to protect you.'

And after? She wanted to ask him about that. What would she do when it was time to leave this wonderful place? When it was time to leave *him*? How would she cope? What would she do? A feeling of panic assailed her. For the first time Lucy thought about afterwards. Tears pricked her eyelids. They would be apart and it would be hell.

'What are you thinking about?' Alex sounded concerned. He touched her chin and tilted it upwards so that he could look straight into her eyes. 'Lucy?'

She was in so deep that she could barely breathe. Another mess. Another mistake. She loved this man with all her heart and he didn't love her.

'I...I was just thinking how hungry I am!' she replied, with a miraculous attempt at lightness. 'Let's go and get something to eat, shall we?'

He held her face for a moment, as if searching for something, then he smiled that gorgeous, slow, sensual smile and Lucy knew it was all right; she had played the part of a relaxed individual and got away with it—for the moment at least.

'Your latest book—what's it about? I've been wanting to ask you.' They were in the kitchen, tucking into a simple feast of bread and cheese that tasted as if it was fit for kings.

'The emotional torment of relationships. Heartache, anguish.' Alex smiled vaguely. 'That sort of thing.'

'A laugh a minute, then?' Lucy teased.

'Hysterical,' he replied with a dry smile.

'Is that why you need that book?' she asked casually.

He frowned. 'Which book are you talking about?'

'You know,' she replied lightly. 'The one on your shelf.'

'There are several hundred books on my shelves,' Alex remarked smoothly. He concentrated on his food for a moment and then added, 'Which one in particular were you referring to?'

His eyes were intense; that was what Lucy noticed the most. She met his gaze and chickened out. She didn't know why; she just did. 'Do you think I could read it some time?' she asked quickly.

'It's not finished.'

'But when it is, then?' she persisted.

'Give it two years and you'll be able to see it on the shelves,' Alex replied lightly.

Realisation dawned. 'You don't *want* me to read it,' she murmured.

'One dark winter's afternoon,' Alex continued relentlessly, 'you'll be out shopping and you'll pass by your local bookshop and you'll notice a sinister-looking cover with my name splashed across the front, and you'll say, "Oh, Alex Darcy! I remember him. I wonder what the cantankerous swine is doing now?"'

'Don't!' Lucy whispered fiercely down at her plateful of food, hanging her head.

'Don't what?' Alex wasn't that obtuse; he knew what she meant. He released a taut breath. 'Look, I'm edgy about my work—you must have discovered that by now. It will only spoil things if I let you read it unfinished— or finished, for that matter. Wait. Time will have passed and—'

'You mean we won't know one another by then, so it won't matter. Our relationship will just be a distant memory.' She struggled to keep her voice even. She looked across at him. 'That's what you're saying, isn't it?'

He hesitated a moment, and then he killed all Lucy's hopes with a nod of his head and a single, solitary syllable. 'Yes.'

'Of course, you're right.' Her voice sounded strained but amazingly strong. She rose from the table and made a great deal of clearing the food from her plate. 'I could be anywhere in two years' time. Alone or with someone. A success or a miserable failure...'

'Never that.' She heard his chair scrape on the stone floor. He walked towards her and she closed her eyes and steeled herself for the first moment of his touch. When it came, though, she still wasn't prepared; it still made her feel like crying. Strong arms wound around her waist, squeezing gently. 'You can achieve or have anything you set your mind to,' he stressed urgently. 'Anything!'

Except you, Lucy thought miserably, turning her head away, resting her cheek on Alex's chest. Anything except that.

CHAPTER NINE

'I'M GOING to see Jeff today.'

'You sound determined.'

Lucy sat up in bed, positioning a pillow behind her head, watching as Alex walked to his wardrobe and selected a shirt to go with the pale chinos that he was already wearing. 'I am. Very.'

'Sounds ominous.' He slipped the crisp blue shirt over his naked torso. Lucy made a conscious effort and dragged her eyes away from the rippling brown muscles. 'And what are you going to tell him?'

'That I'm not interested in acting in his film,' she replied firmly, fixing her gaze on Alex's face. 'That I don't like him, or the way he operates. And that I'm exceedingly glad you knocked him into the pool!'

Alex's mouth curved. 'Just like that?'

She nodded resolutely. 'Yes.'

'He's not going to be too pleased.'

Lucy snuggled further under the cover. She desperately wanted to stay here, safe and warm in Alex's bed. She was putting on a brave face. Inside she dreaded the prospect of telling Jeff exactly what she thought of him. 'I honestly couldn't care less!' she replied airily.

Alex came over and sat down on the bed. His hair was still damp from his shower, slicked back darkly from his face—all except one errant strand. She wanted to reach up and smooth it back for him, but she restrained herself. Little movements like that could give her away, an unasked for caress here, a smile there—Alex would see how she really felt in next to no time.

Since her discovery of Carla's photograph and their conversation of the previous evening, she had decided for the sake of her own sanity that she had to be more contained, more aware of the realities of her situation. She had to combat falling in love with Alex somehow; otherwise the whole situation would turn into one big, embarrassing mess.

OK, so she was hurting inside, but that would be nothing to the humiliation she would have to endure if Alex ever discovered how she really felt. He would be kind. He would explain the impossibility of the situation. And then he would pack her off back to England post-haste and she would never see him again.

If she kept things light, if she acted as if she could handle the superficiality of their relationship, then maybe there would be a chance of something a little more long-lasting. Maybe.

So, this was the new Lucy Harper. Determined and decisive. Making decisions, showing Alex that she was perfectly capable of sorting out her own problems. Feeling just as unsure as she usually did.

'What time shall we leave?'

'Not you.' Lucy shook her head. 'Just me. I want to sort this out on my own.'

Alex frowned. 'Lucy, I don't think—'

'Am I a grown woman or not?' She smiled, but her voice held the necessary warning note. 'I don't need you there holding my hand, Alex. I got myself into this and I can get myself out! I'll get a taxi and it can wait whilst I talk to Jeff; I shouldn't be more than an hour.'

He thought for a moment, dark eyes scanning her face intently. She kept very still, hardly breathing, waiting for his decision. If he insisted on coming she would be more than happy—she no more wanted to face Jeff alone than deal with a poisonous and very slippery snake.

'OK.' He leant forward and dropped a kiss onto her mouth. 'As long as you're sure. I've been a domineering swine on occasions, I know that. It's maybe time I allowed you to stand on your own two feet without interference. But just say what you have to say,' he added firmly, 'and then leave. And don't mention the incident with the swimming pool. Jeff's ego is fragile at the best of times; he won't be too pleased if you start throwing that in his face. Lord knows, he can be a vindictive swine.'

Lucy's heart sank. She was a better actress than she had imagined; she had played the part of a determined woman with a mind of her own rather too well. 'What could he possibly do to me?' she asked scornfully.

'Oh, he won't *do* anything. Jeff's not a great man for action,' Alex responded drily. 'He may say things, though—things that are hurtful. Will you be able to handle that?'

'I've handled a lot worse than Jeff,' she replied quietly. 'Anyway, what's that proverb? "Sticks and stones may break my bones..."' She forced a confident smile. 'Are you trying to put me off on purpose, Alex Darcy? I thought you wanted me to back out of this film!'

'I do! Of course I do.' He kissed her mouth again, only this time his lips lingered seductively. He pulled back after a moment and added, 'I want you to take my mobile phone with you, just in case. If you don't feel up to it, you can punch in a couple of digits and I'll be right there!'

'As long as that's all the punching that's going to get done!' she delivered with a swift smile.

'I just want you to be prepared, that's all,' he told her firmly. 'Not everyone's as sweet and lovely as you.'

His words made her glow. It was the nearest he had come to an endearment and she savoured every syllable. Their kiss resumed and Lucy gave herself up to the ecstasy of it, winding her arms around his neck, thrusting away all her uncertain thoughts.

When she was in his arms she felt powerful, capable of anything. She would do this. She would simply tell Jeff that she had made a mistake, then come back here to Alex and start thinking positively about her life.

Maybe, if Alex saw how assertive she could be, how independent, it would make all the difference to their relationship.

Maybe.

There didn't seem to be a great deal going on when Lucy arrived at the location. But then, she knew that filming was often like this—lots of hanging around being bored, followed by spells of intense and frenetic activity.

Oh, well, at least she had arrived at a good time; that would make her task easier; she needed a few calm moments to speak to Jeff.

She asked the taxi driver to wait in halting Spanish— swiftly learned words that Alex had helped her with just before she'd left—and then scanned the numerous people that were hanging around the jumble of trailers and equipment that littered the beautiful countryside.

Jeff was relatively easy to spot. Another vibrant-coloured shirt proclaimed his presence. He was standing beside the catering truck talking to a waif-like girl with long blonde hair which hung like a golden sheet around her shoulders.

Lucy walked boldly across. She was wearing a cream wrap-around skirt in lightest cotton and a matching halter-neck top—an outfit that she knew she looked good in. She inhaled a deep breath. This was acting, this look of casual confidence. It was just a pity that she didn't feel as good on the inside; her stomach was a churning ball of jelly and her hands were shaking so hard that she had to grip the straps of her bag very tightly so her nerves wouldn't be noticed.

'Jeff!'

He turned at the sound of her voice. There was no smile. Not that she had expected one. The girl turned too. Lucy cast her a swift glance and saw that underneath her wrap she was wearing a very familiar costume...

'Lucy.' Jeff gave a curt nod. 'I didn't expect to see you again. Not after the fiasco I had to endure the other night. Don't tell me Alex has actually allowed you out!'

Lucy steadied herself. There were a million and one things she could say, but she decided, having seen Jeff's belligerent face, to stick to the basics. 'I just wanted to tell you that I'm not interested in continuing with the film.'

'Fine.' Jeff turned and whispered something to the woman at his side, and she left them without a word. 'As you can see, I've worked that out for myself.' He followed the girl's progress with admiring eyes. 'Portia flew out from England yesterday. She's going to be marvellous in the role.'

'Oh . . . oh, I see!' Lucy paused wondering what to say next. 'So you haven't been . . . inconvenienced in any way, then?'

'No more than usual. To tell you the truth, Lucy,' Jeff added, with a false smile that fooled neither of them, 'you were a bit wooden. I decided to give you the benefit of the doubt because . . . well, Alex and I go back a long way, but . . .'

She couldn't let him get away with that. She might be weak and unsure of herself, but for Alex's sake she wouldn't allow Jeff to lie so blatantly. 'You used me.' Lucy's voice was flat. 'I know what happened with Carla. Alex told me.' She had promised him that she would keep it brief and impersonal, but looking at Jeff's artificial expression made her blood boil. 'You used me just to get at him,' she continued frostily. 'He tried to warn me in the beginning, but I wouldn't listen.'

'But you're listening now.'

Lucy inhaled a steadying breath. 'Yes.'

'He's really had an effect, hasn't he?' Jeff drawled. 'Good old Alex. Ever the healer. Mind you, I'm surprised he's taken the treatment as far as he has.' Jeff's mouth curved into an ominous smile. 'You *are* sleeping with him, aren't you?'

'That's none of your—'

'Yes, I know!' he interrupted swiftly. 'It's none of my business! So, how are you feeling?'

Lucy frowned. She didn't understand where the conversation was going. Jeff was playing some sort of game with her but she didn't know what. 'Fine.' She hesitated and then added sharply, 'Why? Shouldn't I be?'

'You've had a few difficulties recently, or so I understand.' Jeff smiled. He paused for effect, holding her attention because she sensed there was more to come. 'The change of scene must have done you good. Lots of warm Mediterranean sunshine—bound to be a tonic. Especially when you've been cooped up inside for several weeks.' Brown eyes held her face with cold precision. 'Never have liked hospitals myself. It's something about the smell. Mind you, the thought of all those nurses in uniform...'

Lucy's stomach flipped over. Nausea rose. 'Who told you?' she whispered.

'Oh, I made a few enquiries,' Jeff drawled. 'Charles Harper's your stepbrother, isn't he? Yeah, well, he came over to lecture at my college in the States a few years back. I was into politics in a big way in those days. We still have a couple of mutual friends.'

'I find that hard to believe!' Lucy replied sharply. 'Charles is extremely choosy about his friends.'

'You've had a rough time,' he continued, ignoring her retort. 'Charles must have been relieved to be able to call on the services of Alex.'

'What are you talking about?' Lucy didn't try to hide her dislike. 'Neither my past nor my relationship with Alex has anything to do with you!' She threw Jeff a disgusted look. 'Alex said you were a vindictive swine; now I can see why!'

'Which relationship are you referring to?' he enquired with a venomous smile. 'The physical one, or the professional one?'

'I don't know what you're talking about! And I don't particularly care!' She began to turn away.

'You don't know, do you?'

Something about Jeff's voice made her turn back. She looked into his smiling face and felt a kind of fear, a swift sensation of foreboding. She frowned irritably, taking a cautious step towards him. 'Know what?'

'Alex hasn't always been a writer. He has other strings to his bow. Didn't your brother tell you?'

'Tell me what?' She released an impatient breath. 'What are you talking about?'

'My, my!' Jeff drawled. 'Alex *has* played his cards close to his chest, hasn't he? But then I've always thought he's a devious devil.'

'Will you just say what you have to say?' Lucy cried angrily. 'I'm sick of all this pathetic innuendo!'

'He's an expert on the mind.' Jeff delivered conversationally. 'Hard to believe it to look at him, I know, but it's one of life's amazing little anomalies. Psychoanalysis. Alex's speciality.' Jeff paused—time enough to allow his words to sink in—then turned the knife in the wound by adding innocently, 'I wonder how much Charles is paying him?'

'No!' It was a harsh whisper—all that Lucy could manage. She stared at Jeff in horrified fascination. He would be enjoying her reaction, she knew, but she couldn't do anything about it. Alex was a...a psychiatrist? Lucy half shook her head. 'I—I don't believe you,' she whispered.

'It's true,' he drawled. 'I may be vindictive, but I'm not an absolute liar—not about that anyway. Ask him yourself if you don't believe me.'

'I will!' She gulped a breath, feeling sick inside. 'Yes...I will!' she repeated helplessly. She turned, unable to bear the look of smug satisfaction on Jeff's face a moment longer, and half ran, half stumbled towards the taxi which was mercifully still waiting for her.

The taxi driver put down his newspaper as she approached and got out of the car, a look of concern on his lined face.

Lucy sat in a daze on the back seat, oblivious to the man's accented enquiry about her health and next destination.

The car chugged into life. Lucy glanced out of the window and caught sight of Jeff's cold expression.

Was it true? She stared ahead in unseeing disbelief. Alex *paid* by Charles to *treat* her? She flinched at the thought, closing her eyes tightly against the possibility. No! No! she cried silently. It couldn't be true—could it?

The taxi driver had assumed that she wanted to return to the villa. It wasn't until the car was bumping along the dusty track that Lucy realised how far they had travelled.

'No!' she said sharply. 'Not here!' She tapped the driver on the shoulder and shook her head, gesturing that he should stop the car. She wasn't ready to face Alex yet—soon, but not yet. She needed some space, time to think things out. Time to compose herself for the possible humiliation that lay ahead.

After an hour the phone rang. Lucy, startled by the odd-sounding noise coming from her leather bag, took a moment to work out what it was.

She held the compact instrument in her hand and stared at it in dismay. It could only be one person. But talking to Alex on the phone would be absolute hell. There was no way she could do it.

The tears that she had held in check for so long began to slide down her cheeks. Lucy scrubbed them away with the back of her hand and pressed one of the buttons. The ringing stopped.

Lucy got up from the shaded rock and walked slowly across the field at the bottom of the orchard. She shaded her eyes against the midday sun and looked up at the villa. She had been circling it from a distance for quite a while, going over and over what she would say and do when she finally found the courage to enter and confront Alex.

Nothing would make any difference. She could rant and rave, or play it as cool as she liked, but if what Jeff had said was true she knew she would have to leave.

'Where the hell have you been? I've been worried about you!'

'Have you?' Lucy glanced sideways at the car and arched a single brow in surprise. 'How comforting.'

'What's the matter?' Alex narrowed his gaze through the driver's window in concerned fashion and Lucy steeled herself for what was to come.

He had come upon her as she walked up the drive. The Jaguar's tyres had screeched behind her, scattering stones and dust as the car had crunched to a halt. 'Did Jeff give you a hard time?' he asked sharply.

'You could say that.'

He watched her, waiting for more. When there was none, Alex said sharply, 'Well? Are you going to tell me what's been going on or not? I went to the location but you weren't there. Jeff said you had told him about not wanting to be in the film and then left almost immediately.'

'So I did,' Lucy murmured.

'Well?' Alex's voice was impatient. He got out of the car and slammed the door shut behind him. 'Where have you been?'

'Just walking.'

Alex searched her face for a moment in silence. 'Why?' he asked evenly.

'Jeff and Charles have mutual friends. Did you know that?' Lucy's voice was tight with suppressed emotion, but she was determined to appear as calm as possible.

'No.' His expression was hawk-like. Very still. Very watchful. 'No, I didn't.'

She walked away from him—just inches of space between them and he let her go. That was a sign of how bad it was, she thought despairingly: he let her go.

'Lucy!'

She had taken four steps. She was hot and bothered and she had an overwhelming desire to sink to her knees, but she inhaled a deep breath and looked back, acknowledging the grim expression on his face. He knew.

Lucy gripped her bag so tightly that her knuckles whitened. 'How could you?' she accused him breathlessly. 'No wonder you felt bad when you took me to bed!'

Alex didn't look puzzled. He didn't ask what on earth she was talking about. He was too sharply intelligent for that. Anguish tore at Lucy's heart. He knew.

'Whatever Jeff's said—'

'Is the truth!' Lucy snapped. 'I only have to look into your face to see that! Well, go on, then!' she added fiercely. 'Stand there and tell me you're not a trained psychiatrist, or psychoanalyst, or whatever it is you are!'

'I can't.' He sounded grim. 'You know I can't.'

Lucy closed her eyes, shaking her head in despair. 'I can't believe I've been such a fool!' she whispered almost inaudibly. 'You told me you met Charles at a conference.' Lucy gulped a breath. 'It was a medical conference, wasn't it?'

Alex nodded. 'Yes. But it was a long time ago. I'm a writer now. I've left that part of my life behind.'

How could he speak so calmly? she wondered. *How?* 'You lied!' she flung at him. 'You and Charles between you. He *wasn't* too busy to have me stay!'

'Look, you're hurt and I don't blame you,' Alex began. 'When you've calmed down, we'll talk things over properly—'

'Don't talk to me like I'm one of your damned patients!' she cried. 'What do you think I've been doing for the last two hours? This is as calm as I'm going to get, believe me!'

'Lucy!' Alex took a step towards her.

'Don't come near me!' she cried out harshly. 'Thanks for the lesson in sexual liberation, but I've learned all I'm ever going to!' Her eyes stung, her throat ached with unshed tears. Alex was standing before her looking more ruggedly handsome than she could bear.

She ran from him. It wasn't what she'd planned. It wasn't the action of a composed, mature individual, but she was past caring.

Lucy's feet slipped and skidded on the dusty track. Her legs ached with the exertion, but she needed to put some space between herself and Alex. She didn't know what she was going to do when she reached the villa; she just had to run and run and try to forget.

Her effort was in vain. Alex caught up with her within seconds. He grabbed her by the arm and spun her round. Smouldering dark eyes bit into her face. 'Charles was concerned about you. He wanted you to have the best possible recuperation!'

'So he called on his old friend and asked for a favour! My God,' Lucy cried breathlessly, 'when I think of how easy it was for you to...to—'

'I understand how you must be feeling,' Alex cut in urgently, 'but don't let Jeff's insinuations turn what we have between us into something bad or cheap.'

'They were more than just insinuations!' Lucy retorted sharply. 'He told me the truth—which is more than you did! Charles employed you to look after me—'

'No!' Alex's restraint finally snapped. His grip tightened; he dragged her towards him. 'No!' he repeated fiercely. 'Never. Never in a million years!

'Look at me,' he commanded when she hung her head. 'Do as I say!' he ordered. He reached out a hand and tilted her chin with none too gentle hands, so that she had to look into his face. 'Five years ago I gave up practising. Carla had died and I felt saddened and angry and cheated, because I'd lost the most wonderful sister in the world. That's when I moved out here. I wrote as a form of therapy at first, then it became the only thing I cared about.' He inhaled a sharp breath. 'Charles isn't employing me,' he insisted sharply. 'You have to believe that!'

'You lied!' Lucy echoed miserably.

'I've never lied to you.' He shook his head. 'OK, so maybe I haven't told you the whole truth, but I've never lied.'

Lucy's voice was scathing. *'Maybe.'*

'What the hell was I supposed to do?' he asked angrily. 'Charles put me in an awkward position. I don't blame him—he was only trying to do what he thought was best. But if I had come clean from the moment I laid eyes on you, what would have been the result? You would have turned on your heel and taken the first flight back to England.'

'At least I would have been saved this humiliation!' Lucy's voice almost broke. She gulped a breath and looked defiant.

'I never, ever set out to hurt you,' Alex said with slow emphasis. 'You have to believe that.'

'Why?' she demanded. 'Why should I believe anything you have to say to me?'

Alex sighed. 'My past profession has no bearing on the relationship we have now,' he said slowly. 'OK, so Charles thought it might help. I didn't. It's irrelevant. Do you understand me?' he gritted. 'Irrelevant.'

'You must have known I would find out sooner or later,' Lucy croaked. 'Can't you understand how I feel? I've been deceived. You and Charles—'

'Forget Charles!' he ordered forcefully. 'He's not important. Let's just concentrate on the problems between the two of us. Everything happened so fast—'

'Didn't it just!' Lucy swallowed the lump in her throat. She couldn't cope with this any longer. Alex was breaking her heart. 'I just want to go home,' she added quietly. 'Away from this place. Back to England—'

'Away from me?'

She forced herself to look into his eyes. She couldn't go on like this. There was no future in this crazy relationship; deep down she knew that. Men like Alex Darcy didn't make commitments to girls like her. 'Yes,' she replied firmly. 'Away from you.' She squared her shoulders and held herself upright. 'Now, if you'd let go of my arm...'

He released her reluctantly. Lucy turned quickly, so that he wouldn't see the tears that were glistening in her eyes, and negotiated the final few metres of the track on legs that were like jelly. She heard the car door open and close behind her. She heard the sound of the engine starting, the crunch of the tyres on gravel. Every noise was like a pain inside her.

Her suitcase was packed in record time. Lucy picked it up and looked around the room that had so delighted her when she had first arrived. She had almost begun to feel as if she belonged here. Almost.

She carried her things to the top of the stairs. Her taxi would be here in a moment and she would have to face saying goodbye to Alex.

The door to the spare room was slightly ajar. She wandered in. This was where she had first made a fool of herself. Sleepwalking. Asking him to kiss her... Her heart turned over at the thought of it.

The tea chest was still pushed against the wall, with a jumble of items spilling from it.

Lucy walked over and idly picked up a heavy volume from amongst the assortment of frames and ornaments. Five minutes, she thought, glancing at her watch, and she'd never see Alex again. Never feel his touch, never see his face...

The book was from his past—another learned tome on the complexities of the mind. Lucy closed the pages with a heavy thud. She didn't need reminding. Her gaze fell to the dark wooden frames. She pulled one out and saw that it wasn't a picture of the countryside or a delicately painted watercolour, but a yellowing piece of paper certifying Alex Darcy's right to practise as a psychiatrist.

Lucy placed the certificate back in the box in dismay and turned towards the door.

Alex was there. Watching her.

'Did I touch these when I was in here that night?' Lucy asked quietly.

'Yes.'

She looked down at the box. Tears misted her eyes.

'You can't leave like this.'

'Can't I?' Her mouth twisted into a painful smile. 'Just watch me!'

'Hell!' Alex's voice vibrated with feeling. 'Lucy, don't look at me as if I'm some sort of ogre,' he growled. 'Have you forgotten how good things are between us? Have you forgotten about the way we make each other feel?'

'Don't!' she cried. She held her hands up, like a shield against his powers. 'Can't you see you're just making things worse?'

Worse?' he echoed disbelievingly. 'How could I possibly make things worse? Not telling you about my past was the worst mistake I could have made!' He released a taut breath. 'But I am not going to apologise for making love to you. I am not going to allow you to leave with Jeff's twisted words echoing in your mind.'

'You're going to have to.'

There was an awful, heart-wrenching silence. Lucy wondered if it was possible to collapse with the strain of a broken heart.

'If you ever need me, you know where I am.'

The pain inside increased. Lucy's eyes stung with tears. 'Yes.'

'What will you do?'

'When I get back to England?' She forced her voice to sound reasonably matter-of-fact. 'Oh, start looking for a job. I'm going to accept Charles's offer of a down payment on a flat. It seems silly to keep refusing.'

'You could always go back to drama school,' he responded. 'It's never too late.'

'I suppose so. Who knows?' she added. 'I could end up acting in one of your films! I'm sure there are a good few psychotic roles which I could really get my teeth into!'

He ignored her desperate attempt at sarcasm. 'You can do anything you set your mind to.' He was being serious. Lucy didn't want that. It only made her feel ten times worse.

'My marriage to Paul...' She swallowed, gulping back the tears. The words were hard to get out, but they needed saying. She'd kept the truth locked inside her for too long. 'It was...a failure.'

'I know.'

Lucy glanced across at him and frowned. 'I was...I was glad when he died,' she blurted out breathlessly. 'We were only together a couple of months, but he made my life a misery.'

'There's no need to feel guilty. You weren't responsible for his death,' Alex murmured.

'But I wanted to be!' she cried. 'At times I wanted to be so much!' She stared across at him, wanting the comfort of his arms so badly that it was like a pain. But he stayed where he was, framed by the doorway, looking at her with a tight, unreadable expression. 'And then he *did* die,' Lucy continued, 'and everyone thought... They thought I was in so much pain.'

She gulped a breath. 'I *was*, but not for the right reasons—the reasons that everyone imagined.' She raised her head and looked at Alex through a mist of tears. 'I can be a good actress, you see,' she added with an attempt at lightness. 'Even Charles thought I was overcome with grief, not guilt.' She sniffed hard. 'But not you,' she added on a broken laugh. 'Not the clever psychiatrist!'

'No.' Alex's voice was almost inaudible. 'Not me.' He looked at her and his expression was a cold, hard mask.

'I was pregnant for a little while,' she announced quietly in rigid tones. 'Just a few weeks. I lost it.'

'Lucy!' He sounded tormented. He took a step forward into the room.

'Don't!' Her voice was harsh. 'I don't want your sympathy!'

'You don't want anything from me, do you?' he gritted.

She shook her head. It seemed to be the only thing left to do. She had been hoping, right up until this moment, that he would say he loved her. It was a silly, juvenile dream that was as far removed from reality as any fairy story.

Stay with me! That was what she wanted him to say. I love you! I can't live without you! She held her breath, waiting, giving him time. But he didn't. Fairy tales. She had never liked them.

A horn sounded. Alex glanced across towards the window. 'That will be your taxi.'

'Yes.' She swallowed the lump in her throat and wondered if she were capable of making it as far as the door without collapsing into floods of tears. 'I'll be down in a minute.'

He turned without a word. Lucy watched as he walked to the top of the stairs and picked up her suitcase. 'You still don't want me to come with you to the airport?' he asked, looking back into the room.

'No!' Her voice was sharp. She worked hard at amending her tone and added more calmly, 'There's absolutely no need. Charles has promised he'll be waiting at the other end.'

That will be bad enough, she thought miserably.

'Did you tell him about the way things have been between us?' Alex asked.

Lucy shook her head. The phone call had been fraught, as it was. Charles hadn't been best pleased to hear that she was coming home straight away. It had taken a very determined-sounding Alex to convince Charles that he should comply with Lucy's wishes.

She had been grateful to Alex for that at least.

Maybe when she got back to England she would manage to feel grateful for the other things he had given her too.

Maybe.

CHAPTER TEN

LUCY plumped up the cushions on the settee, picked up a couple of stray magazines from the floor and then walked through to the hallway to pick up her cape and scarf.

The weather was bitter—one of those dark, dark November days when the cold seeped into your bones and froze you from the inside out.

Her flat was warm and cosy, though. One of the first things that Lucy had had installed when she'd first moved to the top-floor apartment of the large house in north London had been efficient central heating.

There was no need to be cold as well as miserable.

She had tried hard not to, but she still thought about Alex constantly. She despised herself for it, but she couldn't help it. Their relationship had been too powerful. It had meant too much—to her if not to him. Six months on and she still couldn't get Alex Darcy out of her mind.

Not that anyone knew, of course.

Lucy glanced around the comfortable room, which was decorated in varying shades of lemon and jade. What would he think of her progress? For progress had been made—huge strides that would have been unthinkable six months ago, when she had left Majorca and Alex behind.

She had viewed her prospects without enthusiasm, decided that the only thing she was any good at was the one thing she had been trained for, scanned the appropriate stage papers for anything that looked even remotely likely, and then auditioned for every part in sight.

It had entailed hours of waiting in musty corridors and large halls with other girls all as desperate as she was for some kind of chance, but it had been better than sitting in her empty flat dwelling on her mistakes. There had been days, weeks of utter despondency, when she had been turned down yet again because she wasn't the right height, or the colour of her hair was wrong, or simply because there were others who were more capable or more experienced than she.

And now, at last, a breakthrough. Lucy thought once again of her newly acquired part in a BBC costume drama. Oh, how determined she was to make something of it. The character was perfect for her; she would be able to make use of all the emotion that was churning around inside her—lost love and pointless grief were like old friends, and she had vowed she would seize the opportunity with all her heart.

She had to be a success. That was all that was left for her now.

The buzzer to her flat rang just as she was about to open the large front door of the house and go out onto the street. Lucy glanced at her reflection in the hallway mirror and adjusted the black beret she wore, wondering who it could be. She hadn't been long enough in the area to make any friends—just the girls from the flat below and a couple of acquaintances she had met through them.

Lucy pulled open the door.

Her first thought was how strange it was to see him dressed in such smart winter attire. His overcoat was darkest charcoal-grey, his shirt was crisp and white, his tie emerald-green, the colour of her eyes...

'Hello.' Alex's voice was deep and vibrant. Lucy looked at him as if she couldn't quite believe that he was standing there before her, although plainly he was, looking just as powerfully handsome as she remembered.

She gripped the edge of the door for support. Behind Alex, the world went about its business: cars swept by, people carried baskets of shopping, a man washed windows.

They looked at one another in silence for a long moment, then spoke together—the inharmonious sound of Alex's deep, gravelly tone coupled with Lucy's harsh, disjointed voice.

'Aren't you going to say anything?'

'Why are you here?'

She couldn't help the way she sounded. A whole six months of trying not to think about Alex down the drain. Back to square one. Wanting him.

'To see you.' He loomed above her, strong and tanned and full of the heart-stopping vitality that she had tried so desperately hard to forget.

'I was just about to go out.' Lucy kept up the note of harshness in her voice. She couldn't crumble, she couldn't throw herself into his arms and sob onto the lapels of his expensive overcoat just because he had decided, after all this time, to take the trouble to see her.

'So I see.' His gaze took in her beret and her swirling black cape, the fiery, glowing tresses of her hair which hung over one shoulder in a long, curling mass. 'Anywhere important?'

'I'm meeting someone.' She wasn't. She had just been about to go down to the local shop for some much needed provisions, but Alex didn't need to know that. Meeting someone sounded as if she had a life. It sounded as if she didn't care whether he was on her doorstep or not.

'You're looking well.'

She had been thinking the same of him. Exceptionally. Fit and tanned and athletic. No pale face. No tear-rimmed eyes. Clearly, when Lucy had vacated his villa and his life, there had hardly been a hiccup.

'Am I?' Lucy's voice was stiff. Nervous anxiety made her throat go tight. 'How did you find me? Oh, don't bother to answer that,' she added swiftly. 'Charles, of course.'

'Yes.'

'I specifically asked him not to mention where I was.'

'He thought six months was time enough. *I* convinced him it was.'

'Well, I don't think it is.' Lucy decided to be bold— to burn her boats completely so that afterwards, when Alex left, she could at least say to herself that she hadn't acted like a fool. 'As far as I'm concerned six years isn't long enough!'

He searched her face with a frown. 'You don't mean that.'

'I do!'

Alex looked as if he was about to say something more, but he checked himself and said after a tense moment, 'Can I come in?'

Lucy gulped a breath. Panic surged through her veins. She wouldn't be able to keep this pretence up much longer. If Alex crossed the threshold she'd never manage to be strong. 'I . . . I told you,' she stammered, 'I'm just on my way out.'

'Lucy, I'm not in England very often.' Dark eyes pierced her face, and for the first time she saw that Alex was working hard to keep his expression under control. 'I want to see you,' he informed her evenly. 'I *need* to see you.'

She thought of all the responses she could make, strong and weak, good and bad. After a tense moment had passed she gave up the battle of trying to pretend that she didn't care whether she never saw him again and stepped back into the hallway. 'Come in, then,' she said quietly.

The walk upwards to her flat seemed interminable. She had imagined so many meetings, so many scenarios involving herself and Alex over the days and weeks following her flight from Palma airport.

Stupidly, they had possessed elements of hope. In the early days, she had even gone as far as to cherish the possibility that she might be carrying his child. Alex had been responsible with contraception, but, even so, there had been one occasion when passion had taken over and responsibility had flown out of the window.

And there had always been a chance. Or so Lucy had led herself to believe. She had been so desperate to hold onto a part of him. Then had come the evidence that had shown her how silly she had been to dream. No baby. No Alex. Oh, how she had cried. Over and over again, endlessly, far into the night.

As the weeks had passed, and there had been no word or sign, Lucy had begun to be more realistic, even defiant. If he turns up now, she had told herself, I'll be strong and sure. I'll show him how little his appearance means to me.

She had been kidding herself; she knew that now. Just seeing him took her breath away, made her ache inside as if she had been mortally wounded.

Lucy inserted the key into her front door with shaking fingers. Alex was right behind her, not touching her, but she could feel the strength of his presence like a tangible thing. He followed her into the narrow hallway. Lucy stood awkwardly, debating whether to take off her hat and coat—whether that action would reveal how very much she wanted him to stay.

Alex's gaze rested on her wooden face. 'Is this all I get to see?'

'The . . . living room's through here.' She led the way, her movements jerky and uncoordinated—struggling with the door, banging into a piece of furniture as she stood back to let Alex pass.

Calm down! she told herself. Don't let him do this to you.

Dark eyes swept around the room in brief scrutiny, then came to rest on her agonised face. 'I like it.' His voice was deep and resonant, so achingly attractive that Lucy felt pain and had to turn away. 'You've done well. Charles has told me of your recent success.'

That had been another agony—keeping up a strong front for Charles. She knew he still kept in touch with

Alex and it had taken all her strength and determination not to batter Charles with questions about him.

Lucy stood rigidly in front of the fireplace, watching as Alex removed his overcoat. So many times she had dreamed of him standing here, just as he was doing now. So many times...

She inhaled a steadying breath and tried to sound calm. 'Things haven't turned out too badly,' she murmured.

'No?' He looked across at her. 'You must be pleased.'

Was that a question or a statement? Lucy glanced into his enigmatic eyes and then away again. She couldn't be sure. 'Ecstatic,' she replied sarcastically.

Her reply seemed to trigger some sort of release. The controlled look vanished from Alex's face and for the first time she caught a glimpse of the emotion and passion that was simmering below the surface. 'Lucy, I—!'

'Don't!' She held up her hands, shaking her head vehemently. He was angry because she wasn't playing his game of 'let's be friends'. Well, too bad, she thought desperately. She couldn't stand this any more. 'I'm not interested in this... this charade of a conversation!' she flared. 'What do you want? A nice, cosy little chat? Well, I'm sorry, but I'm all out of civilised replies and inane enquiries about the villa and your writing and the weather!' She sucked in a lungful of air.

'Could you go, please? I'm on rather a tight schedule this morning,' she croaked. 'Your conscience is clear,' she added after a shaky pause. 'I'm alive and well and living in a respectable suburb of north London. I have some money and a career and I haven't even seen so much as the outside of a psychiatric ward!' She glared at him, struggling to keep a sob from her voice. 'There! Satisfied?'

'Do you expect me to be?' Alex's voice was low and gritty. She risked a glance and saw that he wasn't bothering to hide any of his anger.

Lucy trembled at the sight of it, but somehow she forced herself to continue. 'Frankly, yes!' She turned from him and walked towards the door. Pride enabled her legs not to buckle beneath her, permitted her fingers to grip the handle and turn it. Not her heart or her head, just stubborn, stupid pride. 'Now, if you'll excuse me...?' She waited, watching with a body that was as rigid as a board.

Alex looked at her, and the intensity of his look made her shiver. There was a strange, almost dangerous silence. 'I love you,' he told her huskily.

Lucy wasn't sure that she had heard correctly. She inhaled a short, swift breath and looked across at him. Her heart was thudding fit to burst. The blood pounded in her ears. She tried to speak, but no words would come. She shook her head, mute, mesmerised by what he had said.

'I love you,' he repeated slowly. 'I can't live without you.'

The silence returned. They looked at one another across the room.

She could hardly believe that he had spoken such wonderful words. It was almost too fantastic; Lucy wanted to rush forward, to throw her arms around his strong, tanned neck, to hold him tight, feel the strength of his body enveloping hers. But if she moved, if she breathed, wouldn't the bubble burst? Wouldn't she wake up and discover it had all been a dream?

'Aren't you going to say anything?' His eyes searched her face, demanding an answer, his voice rough and a little unsteady, just as Lucy's had been, as it still was...

'All...' She took a swift, ragged breath. 'All this time...I thought...I thought there was no hope...' Her voice trailed away. She stood rigidly, unaware of anything except that Alex had told her he loved her and couldn't live without her.

'All this time has not changed anything,' he said huskily. 'I loved you in Majorca.' He paused, and his dark eyes glittered fire and passion and all the intensity of such emotion. 'I love you now.'

'But you let me go!' she whispered, her eyes wide in amazement. 'I thought you didn't care.'

'You were angry. You hated me.' Lucy shook her head, but Alex continued roughly, 'You *looked* as if you hated me. I gazed into your eyes and I could see all the hurt and the misery. *I* did that to you.' He shook his head as if he could hardly believe it. 'I felt so... inadequate. I'd made you unhappy and I couldn't forgive myself. You told me you wanted to leave,' he added after a ragged pause. 'I punished myself by agreeing that you should go.'

'You punished me, too.'

'But I thought it was what you wanted. You were so determined—' Alex began.

'Only because I thought it was what *you* wanted!' Lucy retorted. She shook her head. 'I felt humiliated, confused. When Jeff told me those things—'

'They weren't true!' Alex cut in feverishly. 'You surely know that by now?'

'Charles did tell me how it really was,' she murmured. 'He was very sorry that he had helped cause a disagreement between us.'

'A *disagreement*?' His voice held something approaching wonder. 'You never asked about me,' he added slowly. 'Charles thought you would...' Dark eyes held her face. 'So did I.'

'What was the point?' she whispered. 'I thought you didn't care. It would only have been painful. When Jeff told me Charles had paid you to... look after me, it was as if all my worst nightmares had come true. It was as if... as if I had been expecting it. I couldn't quite believe that you found me attractive for myself.'

'Paul really destroyed all your self-belief, didn't he?' Alex murmured quietly.

Lucy looked at him and nodded. 'Yes,' she whispered. 'I've never been particularly confident.'

'You didn't imagine I could possibly love you. Is that what you're trying to say?'

'Yes. I had been hoping, of course. You were so...intense when we were together. But I didn't dare allow myself to truly believe.'

'I should have told you.' His voice was full of torment. She looked across at him. 'Why didn't you?'

He dragged a hand through his dark hair and shook his head—a gesture that portrayed irritated disbelief. 'Because I was a fool. I had never experienced anything that had come close to the way you made me feel. I was astonished, unsure of myself in relation to you. Nervous. Shell-shocked. I thought I had my life under control. I thought I had everything planned out.'

Alex shook his head again. 'I also didn't want to burden you with my baggage of emotions. You had told me you wanted to keep things simple and I forced myself to go along with it.' He managed a self-deprecating smile. 'Well, I tried, anyway. It wasn't particularly easy.' Dark eyes bored into Lucy's face like hot, blazing coals. 'I should never have let you see Jeff alone like that. He said some terrible things.'

'I should never have believed him. You told me what he was like. I should have trusted you. Deep down I knew that I was overreacting,' Lucy added. 'I wanted to understand the way it really was, but I didn't have the courage to believe that you liked me purely for myself. I was afraid. You talk about punishment. Well, my punishment was not allowing myself to hope, or to cherish all the good things we had between us.' Her voice came to a shaky halt. She inhaled a steadying breath and forced herself to continue. 'We had passion. We had desire. I wasn't sure if we had love.'

'But you're sure now?'

Lucy smiled. She wanted to throw her arms around his neck. She wanted to touch him so much! He looked so wonderful standing there. The most handsome, most intensely passionate man she had ever known, ever *wanted* to know. And he loved her. She could scarcely believe it.

'Yes.' She forced herself to hold onto restraint for a little while longer. 'But six months is a long time.'

'Tell me about it.' Alex's expression held torment. 'Every day,' he murmured. 'Every single day I thought about you.'

'Why so long?' she asked quietly. 'If you loved me—'

'Don't you see? It's because I loved you that I let you go. You needed time and space to work things out, to build your own life. To get your marriage to Paul out of your system, maybe to get me out too...' He looked at her and his dark eyes glittered. 'Has there been anyone else?'

He was the one in torment. That Alex could look so...so haunted and ask that question... 'No!' Lucy shook her head and allowed herself the biggest, brightest smile the world had ever seen. 'Oh, Alex!' She sobbed as she spoke his name. 'I love you so much! Every day...every hour... I can't survive another minute without you!'

She ran to him then and he opened his arms and held her fiercely, as if she were a lifeline and he never wanted to let her go.

Their kiss was a clash of mouths, hungry and searching, overflowing with the frenzy of desire. Alex tugged her beret from her head, ran his fingers through the endless strands of glowing hair, held her face, kissed every part of it, dragged the cape from her shoulders, felt beneath for the curves of her breasts and hips, his powerful hands stroking the long lines of her thighs, moving up to caress the fragility of her throat.

'I want you now!'

His voice made her heart sing. In all her life she would never forget this moment. Such sweet intensity because of the agony of time spent apart.

The floor served as a bed. They lay upon it before the flickering embers of the fire. The room held its breath as impatient fingers dragged away unnecessary garments and limbs entwined with frantic intensity.

Lucy looked up into Alex's face, her emerald eyes glowing with love as he paused a moment to observe the beauty of her pale, naked body. 'I can never live without you,' he murmured in hushed tones. 'Never.'

She pulled him towards her in reply, holding his dark head in her hands, pressing her lips against his firm mouth, kissing him over and over again.

And then Alex took control, and Lucy found herself groaning with each exquisite touch and movement. Her body strained and arched towards the force of rippling muscle and smooth, tanned skin. He took possession of her body and it was as if they were making love for the first time—every thrust of his loins a proclamation of love, every gasp and groan from Lucy's lips a sign that she could never live without him.

They lay afterwards in silence, spent and exhausted, just touching, looking, feeling the intensity of their love for one another.

'I never want us to be apart again.'

Alex smiled and touched her face. 'Neither do I.'

'I could be pregnant,' she whispered, smiling.

Dark eyes glowed. 'You wouldn't mind?'

She shook her head. 'Of course not. I love you. I want to have your baby.'

'Makes me happy. Marry me first.'

'Marry you?' Lucy smiled and released a breath. 'Oh, Alex!' Tears filled her eyes. 'You mean it?'

'More than you'll ever know.'

'Yes.' Her emerald eyes widened with desire. She stroked her hands across his chest, along the line of his thigh, touching him as intimately as he had touched her.

'Do you know how much I want to make love to you again?' Alex growled. 'Do you know what you do to me?'

Lucy's lips curved into a sensuous smile. 'I think so,' she murmured. 'But show me anyway.'

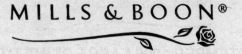

MILLS & BOON®

SEPTEMBER 1996 HARDBACK TITLES

Romance

The Trophy Wife *Rosalie Ash*	H4516	0 263 14938 2
Honeymoon Assignment *Sally Carr*	H4517	0 263 14939 0
Meant to Marry *Robyn Donald*	H4518	0 263 14941 2
No More Secrets *Catherine George*	H4519	0 263 14942 0
Rebel in Disguise *Lucy Gordon*	H4520	0 263 14943 9
Where There's a Will *Day Leclaire*	H4521	0 263 14944 7
Aunt Lucy's Lover *Miranda Lee*	H4522	0 263 14946 3
Daddy's Little Helper *Debbie Macomber*	H4523	0 263 14947 1
Living With the Enemy *Laura Martin*	H4524	0 263 14948 X
One-Man Woman *Carole Mortimer*	H4525	0 263 14949 8
His Sleeping Partner *Elizabeth Oldfield*	H4526	0 263 14951 X
Jilted Bride *Elizabeth Power*	H4527	0 263 14952 8
First-Time Father *Emma Richmond*	H4528	0 263 14953 6
Desert Wedding *Alexandra Scott*	H4529	0 263 14954 4
Dominic's Child *Catherine Spencer*	H4530	0 263 14964 1
Once Burned *Margaret Way*	H4531	0 263 14965 X

Historical Romance™

The Rainborough Inheritance *Helen Dickson*	M391	0 263 15015 1
The Last Gamble *Mary Nichols*	M392	0 263 15016 X

Medical Romance™

The Ideal Choice *Caroline Anderson*	D309	0 263 15001 1
More than Skin-Deep *Margaret O'Neill*	D310	0 263 15002 X

MILLS & BOON®

SEPTEMBER 1996 LARGE PRINT TITLES

Romance

Last Stop Marriage *Emma Darcy*	935	0 263 14712 6
Husband Material *Emma Goldrick*	936	0 263 14713 4
The Colorado Countess *Stephanie Howard*	937	0 263 14714 2
A Simple Texas Wedding *Ruth Jean Dale*	938	0 263 14715 0
Untamed Lover *Sharon Kendrick*	939	0 263 14716 9
Relative Sins *Anne Mather*	940	0 263 14717 7
A Faulkner Possession *Margaret Way*	941	0 263 14718 5
A Night to Remember *Anne Weale*	942	0 263 14719 3

Historical Romance™

Farewell the Heart *Meg Alexander*	0 263 14776 2
A Biddable Girl? *Paula Marshall*	0 263 14777 0

Medical Romance™

And Daughter Makes Three *Caroline Anderson*	0 263 14726 6
A Question of Trust *Maggie Kingsley*	0 263 14727 4
The Disturbing Dr Sheldon *Elisabeth Scott*	0 263 14728 2
Consultant Care *Sharon Wirdnam*	0 263 14729 0

TEMPTATION™

A Kiss in the Dark *Tiffany White*	0 263 14962 5
Undercover Baby *Gina Wilkins*	0 263 14963 3

MILLS & BOON®

OCTOBER 1996 HARDBACK TITLES

ROMANCE

Married for Real *Lindsay Armstrong*	H4532	0 263 14975 7
A Wife for Christmas *Pamela Bauer & Judy Kaye*		
	H4533	0 263 14981 1
Their Wedding Day *Emma Darcy*	H4534	0 263 14976 5
The Final Proposal *Robyn Donald*	H4535	0 263 14977 3
All She Wants for Christmas *Liz Fielding*	H4536	0 263 14978 1
Torn by Desire *Natalie Fox*	H4537	0 263 14979 X
Trouble in Paradise *Grace Green*	H4538	0 263 14980 3
His Baby! *Sharon Kendrick*	H4539	0 263 14982 X
Because of the Baby *Debbie Macomber*	H4540	0 263 14983 8
Powerful Persuasion *Margaret Mayo*	H4541	0 263 14984 6
Bad Influence *Susanne McCarthy*	H4542	0 263 14985 4
Angel Bride *Barbara McMahon*	H4543	0 263 14986 2
The Vicar's Daughter *Betty Neels*	H4544	0 263 14988 9
Mistletoe Man *Kathleen O'Brien*	H4545	0 263 14987 0
Unexpected Engagement *Jessica Steele*	H4546	0 263 14989 7
Borrowed Wife *Patricia Wilson*	H4547	0 263 14990 0

HISTORICAL ROMANCE™

His Lordship's Dilemma *Meg Alexander*	M393	0 263 15085 2
An Affair of Honour *Paula Marshall*	M394	0 263 15086 0

MEDICAL ROMANCE™

A Wish for Christmas *Josie Metcalfe*	D311	0 263 15073 9
Wings of Duty *Meredith Webber*	D312	0 263 15074 7

MILLS & BOON®

OCTOBER 1996 LARGE PRINT TITLES

ROMANCE

The Right Choice *Catherine George*	943	0 263 14746 0
For the Love of Emma *Lucy Gordon*	944	0 263 14747 9
The Desert Bride *Lynne Graham*	945	0 263 14748 7
Only by Chance *Betty Neels*	948	0 263 14751 7
The Morning After *Michelle Reid*	949	0 263 14752 5
Working Girl *Jessica Hart*	946	0 263 14749 5
The Lady's Man *Stephanie Howard*	947	0 263 14750 9
White Lies *Sara Wood*	950	0 263 14753 3

HISTORICAL ROMANCE™

A Fragile Mask *Elizabeth Bailey*	0 263 14828 9
Katherine *Helen Dickson*	0 263 14829 7

MEDICAL ROMANCE™

Bush Doctor's Bride *Marion Lennox*	0 263 14764 9
Forgotten Pain *Josie Metcalfe*	0 263 14765 7
Country Doctors *Gill Sanderson*	0 263 14766 5
Courting Dr Groves *Meredith Webber*	0 263 14767 3

TEMPTATION®

Baby Blues *Kristine Rolofson*	0 263 15019 4
Ghost Whispers *Renee Roszel*	0 263 15020 8